PHAT GIRL

JAY VINCENT JONES

(PHAT GIRL) may be ordered through booksellers or by contacting:
JVJPublishing
1440 W Taylor Street Suite 1039
Chicago, IL 60607
jvjpublishing@gmail.com
(312) 373-0276

ISBN: 978-1-7335997-6-4 (sc)

copyright date 04/01/2026
JVJ Publishing First release date: 04/10/2026
Cover art by: Jay V. Jones

CONTENTS

INTRODUCTION

"I'm tired of being the biggest one everywhere I go. I'm tired of pretending I'm okay with it. I'm tired of trying to love myself when half the time I don't even like myself."

PROLOGUE

She bought new clothes, nicer ones, pieces that felt more expensive against her skin. She studied makeup tutorials and practiced blending foundation until her arm hurt. She switched her perfume to something warmer, something that promised confidence in its description. She began waking up earlier for morning walks, blending smoothies, writing short affirmations she barely believed.

But every night, after she undressed and washed her face, she felt exactly the same.

Still invisible.

Still overlooked.

Still… Kayla.

1

THE POWER OF FRIENDSHIP

While standing in front of her full-length mirror, Kayla tugged at her dress, and forced herself to look. The woman staring back at her wasn't a stranger. She knew this body: the soft, generous curves, the full cheeks that puffed when she laughed, the brown skin that people always said was "so pretty," like it was an accessory and not part of her. Her locs were pulled into a high bun, a few loose strands framing her face. Her makeup was subtle—gold on her eyelids, gloss on her lips. She looked...nice.

She also felt like screaming.

"Okay, Kay," she whispered to her reflection. "Mask on."

She straightened her shoulders, pulled the wrap dress a little tighter around her waist, and gave the mirror what everyone else saw —a bright, confident smile that made people say things like, You always light up the room and Girl, I wish I had your energy.

Nobody ever said, I see how lonely you are.

Her phone buzzed on the dresser. The group chat, titled, "Feast & Talk Queens," lit up the screen.

Lisa: Y'all, I'm starving. Did anybody die today so we can cancel or nah?

Michelle: I'm already in the car. And I look too cute to cancel.

Jasmine: On my way. Kayla better have my chair ready.

Sarah: 22 minutes away. If the food not hot by the time I get there, I'm writing all of you out of my will.

Kayla smiled for real this time. Her girls always knew how to pull her out of her head.

Kayla: Food's ready. And yes, Jas, your seat is waiting. Don't be late or Michelle's taking your chicken.

From the kitchen, the smell of garlic, butter, and roasted herbs drifted down the hallway. She'd gone overboard again—baked chicken, creamy mashed potatoes, roasted vegetables, macaroni and cheese, cornbread, and a big bowl of salad that the girls would pretend to eat. "We love balance," they always joked.

Kayla checked the dining table one more time. Plates, forks, cloth napkins folded into neat little triangles. Candles burning in simple glass jars. A bouquet of sunflowers from the grocery store sitting in a mason jar in the center.

It wasn't fancy, but it felt warm. It felt like them.

The doorbell rang.

"Coming!" she called, smoothing her dress one last time before heading to the door.

She opened it to a whirlwind of red curls, perfume, and chaos.

"Baby!" Lisa practically sang, stepping into the apartment like she owned the building. "Do you know I almost fought your security guard downstairs? He told me my parking was illegal. I told him my existence is illegal. Now where's the food?"

Lisa was exactly who people pictured when they imagined a woman who ran a marketing department at a downtown Chicago firm: tailored coat in winter white, lipstick that matched nothing and somehow matched everything, heels high enough to cause injuries. Her curly red hair framed her pale face, and her green eyes sparkled with a constant mix of sarcasm and mischief.

"Hi, Lisa," Kayla said, laughing. "You know some people say hello before demanding chicken."

"Some people ain't been in meetings with ugly men all day. I deserve carbs and comfort." Lisa kissed Kayla's cheek in greeting, then sniffed the air. "Mac and cheese? I knew it. Your love language."

"Food is everybody's love language," Kayla replied. "You know where your wine glass is."

Before Lisa could respond, the door swung wider, and Jasmine rushed in, juggling a tote bag, a pan of store-bought brownies, and her car keys.

"Don't judge me," Jasmine said, holding up the brownies. "I had three employee meltdowns, two managers lying to my face, and one termination today. You're lucky I brought anything."

Jasmine had the kind of presence that made people spill their secrets. Her deep brown skin glowed, and she wore her thick hair pulled into a sleek ponytail. Even in jeans and a simple blouse, she gave off "assistant director of HR" energy—competent, composed, but always one step away from a dramatic eye roll.

"Girl, you know we'll eat those brownies like you baked them from scratch," Kayla said, taking the pan. "Stress level that bad?"

"Let's just say I earned every crumb," Jasmine replied, kicking off her flats and slipping into the house slippers Kayla kept by the door. "Where's Michelle? She's always early when food's involved."

"Already at my stove," Kayla said.

Sure enough, when they walked into the kitchen, Michelle was there, hip-bumped against the counter, stirring something on the stove that Kayla had clearly finished already.

"Don't touch my gravy," Kayla warned.

"Too late," Michelle replied, licking a spoon. "Your gravy's flirting with me. I had to respond."

Michelle was a walking art exhibit: bright patterns, bold earrings, flawless eyeliner. Her dark brown skin glowed against the yellow jumpsuit she'd squeezed herself into. A graphic designer by day, a professional "extra" by nature, she saw the world in colors and shapes—and turned everything into a story.

"You look like sunshine," Kayla said.

"I know." Michelle winked. "I'm doing color therapy on myself. My boss sent me a 'quick edit' at 4:58 pm That man is a demon."

"Okay, so we're all traumatized," Lisa announced, pouring wine into stemless glasses. "Where's Sarah? She's usually here early so she can judge everybody's financial decisions over dinner."

"Five minutes out," Jasmine said, glancing at her phone. "She just texted, 'Parking. If I get towed, I'm billing you all.'"

They were halfway through setting dishes on the table when the door opened again.

"You left it unlocked," Sarah called from the hallway. "Clearly, you trust your neighbors too much."

"Hey, mama," Kayla said, peeking around the corner.

Sarah stepped into the dining room, hanging her coat with deliberate care. Where Lisa embodied chaotic sophistication, Sarah was precise. Her blonde hair was pulled into a low bun, not a strand out of place. She wore a simple black dress and low heels, looking like she could walk straight into a board meeting or a funeral without changing a thing.

"Smells amazing," Sarah said. "Did you overdo it again?"

"Probably," Kayla said.

"So…yes," Sarah replied, a small smile finally breaking through her reserved expression. "Good. I brought wine. The expensive one. Don't chug it."

They sat around the table like they always did—Lisa and Michelle across from each other, Jasmine to Kayla's left, Sarah to her right. The first few minutes were always the same: passing dishes, praising Kayla's cooking, pretending the salad was a serious part of the meal.

"So," Lisa said, after a few bites of chicken. "Let's get to the important part. Who's got man drama?"

"No hello? No 'how was your week?'" Sarah deadpanned.

"We just covered that. Everybody's traumatized," Lisa said. "Now I need entertainment."

"My man drama is that I don't have one," Michelle said. "Next."

"You say that like it's a bad thing," Sarah replied. "Single means no one gets on your nerves."

"Liar," Michelle said. "You love when someone gets on your nerves. Gives you a reason to text us paragraphs."

They all laughed.

Kayla watched them, sipping her wine. This was what she lived for —their voices overlapping, the jokes, the way they could be brutally honest and still, so very soft with each other. It made her feel safe. It also reminded her how much she wanted more.

"How about you, Jas?" Lisa said. "Any office romances I should be worried about?"

"Please," Jasmine scoffed. "I'm too busy breaking up other people's relationships in HR meetings. That's enough drama. Besides, dating coworkers is messy."

"You say that like you haven't thought about it," Michelle teased.

Jasmine didn't answer right away. She pushed her mashed potatoes around with her fork.

"There's this new project manager," she admitted. "Tall, smile for days, smells good. But he follows all the rules. Even asked me what the policy was on dating coworkers."

"And you told him…?" Lisa prompted.

"I told him to read the manual," Jasmine replied, and they all groaned.

"Jasmine," Kayla said, laughing, "you are a hater of your own blessings."

"I am a protector of my paycheck," Jasmine corrected. "Y'all not about to see me on somebody's LinkedIn 'Open to Work' because I was making bad choices at the company picnic."

"I respect that," Sarah said. "Barely, but I respect it."

"What about you, Sarah?" Michelle asked, pointing her fork at her. "You've been real quiet."

Sarah shrugged. "There's a guy at work. Smart, kind, also obsessed with work. We go to lunch, we talk numbers and investments. It's nice. It's also… safe. Too safe."

Lisa narrowed her eyes. "Translation: he bores your underwear off."

"Exactly," Sarah said, and everyone laughed again.

They turned to Kayla.

"What about you?" Jasmine asked. "Anybody caught your eye?"

Kayla opened her mouth, then closed it. She hadn't told them about the man at the coffee shop yet—the tall, broad-shouldered guy in a fitted suit, reading a thick book, who had glanced up at her and smiled. She'd panicked, ducked behind her laptop, and pretended to be invisible.

Typical.

"Nobody serious," she said instead. "Just work. Clients. Soy candles and serums."

"Your skincare business is gonna get you a man before these dating apps do," Michelle said. "You'll have somebody falling in love with you over an exfoliating scrub."

"Well, his skin will at least be happy," Kayla said.

"And his girlfriend too," Lisa added. "If she exists."

They were joking, but the words pressed against something tender in Kayla's chest. She'd become very good at laughing through moments like this.

"Speaking of," Sarah said, changing the subject, "how's your product line going? Any updates?"

Kayla sat back a little, glad for the shift. "Good, actually. I've got three regular spa clients now who order in bulk. And one of my cocoa butter bars went viral on TikTok last week. Some influencer did a 'body care routine' video and I was tagged about a hundred times."

"Excuse me? And you are just now mentioning this?" Lisa demanded. "Send me the link. I'm pitching your brand at my next client meeting. Y'all marketing people love a homemade success story."

Kayla felt heat rise to her cheeks. "It's not that big yet."

"Yet," Sarah echoed. "You know what you should do? Set up a budget and timeline for scaling. You've got demand. Be ready before it blows up."

"And when you're ready to design packaging that looks as good as your products, guess who you're calling?" Michelle said, pointing at herself.

"And when your business gets big enough that HR is a nightmare, call me," Jasmine added.

"And when you need someone to remind you not to give your products away for free to every man with nice teeth, call me," Lisa said.

Kayla laughed so hard she had to put her fork down. "Y'all are ridiculous."

"Correct," Lisa said. "But seriously, girl, we believe in you. You've been talking about your own skincare line since forever. Look at you now."

Kayla swallowed around the unexpected lump in her throat. Compliments were easy to give, hard to receive. It always felt like she had to brace herself before letting them sink in.

"Thanks," she said softly.

For a while they just ate, talked about work, complained about coworkers, and argued about which reality show was currently rotting their brains the most. The room hummed with familiarity. Kayla loved that they didn't tiptoe around the hard stuff, but they never let it swallow the night.

Later, after the dishes were cleared and the wine bottle was half empty, they moved to the living room. Kayla's couch and two mismatched chairs made a rough circle around the coffee table, which now held brownies, grapes, chips, and a bowl of M&M's.

"So," Jasmine said, tucking her feet under her. "Real question. If you could go back and tell your sixteen-year-old self one thing, what would it be?"

Lisa groaned. "Ugh. Are we doing therapy tonight? I didn't bring my co-pay."

"Answer the question," Jasmine said.

"I would tell her," Lisa said dramatically, "to stop dating boys who wear basketball shorts year-round. They have nothing to offer you but heartbreak and ashy knees."

They screamed with laughter.

"What about you, Michelle?" Kayla asked.

Michelle stared at the ceiling for a moment. "I'd tell her that being 'too much' is only a problem for people who are not enough. You know how many times I made myself smaller in high school so boys wouldn't feel intimidated? For what? Those same boys are now in my DMs asking for free logos."

"And you say?" Lisa asked.

"'My hourly rate is $150,'" Michelle replied. "Therapy."

"I like that," Sarah said. "I'd probably tell mine, 'You don't have to be perfect to be loved.' I spent so long thinking if I made one mistake, people would leave."

Jasmine nodded. "I'd tell mine to stop trying to save everybody. Some people like drowning."

They all looked at Kayla.

"And you?" Jasmine asked quietly.

Kayla hesitated. The easy answer was something funny. There was always a joke ready to go. But looking at the women around her—their faces open, waiting—she decided to risk a little more.

"I'd tell her," Kayla said slowly, "that she's not ugly. That the problem was never her body. It was other people's eyes."

The room went quiet for a heartbeat.

Then Michelle slid closer on the couch and bumped Kayla's shoulder with her own. "Amen."

"You were beautiful then, you're beautiful now," Jasmine said. "I'm glad sixteen-year-old you has thirty-something-year-old us."

"And our wine," Lisa added. "Don't forget that."

They laughed again, but the mood had shifted. Something had softened.

Kayla leaned back into the couch, letting the sound of her friends' voices wash over her. Outside, the city went on without them—cars honking, trains rumbling past, people going somewhere, leaving someone, chasing something.

Inside, in her small but warm apartment, she had everything she'd once prayed for: women who saw her, who didn't ask her to shrink or disappear. Women who believed in her dreams even on the days she didn't.

Later that night, after everyone had gone home and the apartment was quiet again, Kayla stood alone in the living room, looking at the empty glasses and crumb-filled plates. The faint echo of their laughter still lingered in the walls.

She tidied up on autopilot, mind drifting. Her life was...good. She had a solid job, a growing business, a circle of women most people would kill for.

So why did she still feel a hollow space inside, like something important was missing?

She turned off the lights and headed to her bedroom. On her dresser, her laptop sat open, the last thing she'd searched still on the screen.

"Skincare manufacturing small batch. How to scale."

She smiled faintly. One day, she thought. One day, these little jars and lotions might sit on shelves in big stores with bright lights. One day, she might walk in and see her name on a label.

And maybe, one day, she'd meet someone who looked at her the way she looked at her dreams—soft, hungry, without doubt.

For now, she had her girls. Her Sunday feasts. Her candles and spreadsheets. Her reflection in the mirror that she was trying to make peace with, one day at a time.

Kayla turned off the screen, climbed into bed, and pulled the covers up to her chin. Her phone buzzed one last time.

Michelle: Love you, sis. Food was bomb. You are bomb. Don't forget it.

Jasmine: Get some rest. You work too hard.

Lisa: Also, your garlic mash almost made me propose.

Sarah: Proud of you. For everything. Good night.

Kayla stared at the messages, that old familiar ache swelling in her chest. This time, she let herself feel it and the gratitude layered on top of it.

"Mask off," she whispered into the dark.

A tear slipped down her cheek. Then another. She let them fall, just for a minute.

Then she wiped her face, took a deep breath, and closed her eyes.

Tomorrow, she'd put the mask back on. She'd go to work, send client emails, label jars of body butter. She'd laugh, listen, and hold everyone else together.

But tonight, alone in her room, she let herself simply be Kayla—soft, imperfect, unfinished.

Somewhere out there, life was already moving pieces she couldn't see yet. A man she hadn't met. A moment in a coffee shop. A stranger's eyes locking with hers.

For now, she slept. And the city kept breathing around her.

2

WHERE LOYALTY LIVES

Kayla woke up before the sun, the quiet kind of morning where the world felt gentle enough not to demand anything from her yet. She stretched, checked her phone, and rolled her eyes.

Three unread messages from her boss.

Six in the morning.

On a Saturday.

She whispered into her pillow, "The man needs a hobby… or a woman."

Across the apartment, in the guest room, she heard Michelle humming — off-key, but upbeat in that naturally bright way she came wired. Michelle was already dressed for her shift at the nonprofit clinic: navy scrubs, curly hair pinned back, coffee in her hand the size of a small bucket.

"Morning, sunshine," Michelle called, sticking her head into Kayla's doorway. "You up, or you just scrolling?"

"Both," Kayla said, sitting up. "My boss is allergic to boundaries."

"Well," Michelle shrugged, "you're allergic to unemployment, so text him back."

Kayla grabbed a pillow and threw it. "Get out."

Michelle laughed and dodged it. "Love you too. Breakfast is on the stove. Eggs, turkey sausage, and whatever's left of that fruit you pretend you're gonna finish."

The apartment door clicked behind her, leaving Kayla in a quiet she didn't hate, just… felt.

She slowly padded to the kitchen where steaming food waited under a foil cover. Michelle always cooked like somebody's mom — nurturing even when she didn't try. Kayla sat at the counter, fork in hand, mind drifting to last night's conversation with Jasmine.

The loyalty talk.

The man problems talk.

The "girl, you deserve better" talk.

Jasmine, corporate strategist, always calm, always polished, and always right in ways Kayla didn't want to admit.

Her voice still echoed in Kayla's head:

"You pour into people who don't pour back. That's not loyalty, Kay. That's draining yourself because you're scared they'll leave if you don't."

Kayla stabbed a piece of pineapple harder than necessary.

"Not wrong," she whispered.

Her phone buzzed again — a text from Jasmine this time.

Jasmine: Morning. Don't forget lunch today. And don't cancel on me like you like to do when your boss stresses you out.

Kayla: I'm coming. Promise.

Jasmine: Good. I'll choose the restaurant. Don't argue.

Kayla smiled. With Jasmine, there was no room for chaos. Everything had structure, intention, order. Kayla needed that more than she admitted.

She showered, dressed in fitted slacks and a soft beige sweater — subtle, stylish, but not trying too hard. Chicago weather didn't allow for anything light anyway.

As she applied her makeup, soft gold shadows and muted browns, she studied her own eyes in the mirror. They looked tired in that emotional way, the kind sleep couldn't fix.

"You are fine," she whispered to herself, then paused.

"No, you will be fine."

By noon, she arrived at Solstice, the downtown restaurant Jasmine loved for its clean lines and overpriced salads. Michelle was already there too — she somehow always beat traffic like she had a personal arrangement with the streets.

Jasmine waved them over from a corner booth, long braids cascading down her back, gold hoops catching the light as she tilted her head with that signature smirk.

"Well," Jasmine said as they sat down, "look who actually showed up on time."

Kayla rolled her eyes. "Funny."

Michelle leaned in. "Can we get menus before she starts lecturing? I'm starving."

The waiter appeared instantly — Jasmine clearly had a regular's pull. They ordered their usuals: grilled salmon salad for Jasmine, pasta for Michelle , and a chicken flatbread for Kayla.

Once the waiter left, Jasmine folded her hands on the table.

"So," she began, "we're gonna talk about yesterday."

Kayla groaned. "Can we not?"

Michelle sipped her iced tea. "We absolutely can."

Kayla glared at both of them. "Why am I being jumped?"

"Because we love you," Michelle said, leaning her chin on her hand. "And when your work life is toxic, your dating life follows right behind like an untrained puppy."

Jasmine nodded. "Exactly. And right now, both are messy."

Kayla slumped. "I'm fine."

"You're functioning," Jasmine corrected softly. "But you're not fine."

The words landed heavier than Kayla expected. She glanced down at her hands.

Michelle touched her wrist gently. "What's going on with you and Marcus?"

Kayla hesitated.

Her chest tightened.

The truth tried to slip out, then stalled.

"Nothing," she said too quickly.

Jasmine's eyes narrowed. "Kayla. Spill."

Kayla looked between them — her sisters in every way that mattered. She swallowed.

"He hasn't called," she said quietly. "It's been three weeks."

Michelle froze. "Three— Kayla, what?"

"And when he did text," Kayla continued, voice fading, "he said he was just 'busy.' Like that's supposed to make me feel special."

Jasmine shook her head slowly. "Kay… no."

Kayla tried to laugh it off, but her chest ached. "I know. I know. I'm stupid."

"Hey." Michelle 's tone sharpened. "Don't do that. You're not stupid."

"You're loyal," Jasmine said. "But you give loyalty like it's oxygen. People have to earn that."

Kayla nodded, blinking too fast. She hated crying in public. She hated crying, period.

"I just thought…" She paused. "I just thought he saw me."

Michelle squeezed her hand under the table. "We see you. And we're not going anywhere."

Their food arrived, interrupting the heaviness just long enough for Kayla to breathe. They ate, laughed at old stories, teased each other, shifted the conversation back to lighter ground.

But as they left the restaurant, Jasmine looped her arm around Kayla.

"You're gonna be okay," she murmured. "And we're not letting you go through anything alone."

Kayla leaned her head on Jasmine's shoulder for a second, letting herself feel it — the real kind of love, not the half-effort attention Marcus threw her way.

For the first time in weeks, Kayla felt something shift inside her.

A small, hopeful breath.

A reminder:

Loyalty doesn't live where it isn't returned.

3

GIRLS, MEN, AND THE MESS BETWEEN

Sunday's brunch at her home was just like church, for the ones who didn't quite make it to church, Kayla always said.

By seven o'clock, her condo smelled like garlic, butter, and every bad decision a nutritionist would warn you about. Shrimp and grits bubbled on the stove, mac and cheese was in the oven doing that slow, holy bake, and a pan of honey–hot wings waited under foil, sweating in their own sauce. The TV murmured some reality show she wasn't even watching; her playlist—90s R&B and a little neo-soul—set the real mood.

She wiped her hands on a towel and glanced at the full-length mirror in the hallway. The same one that caught her on nights when she picked herself apart. Tonight, she tilted her head, pressed her lips together.

"Okay, sis," she whispered to her reflection. "Big girl magic. Smile."

She adjusted her wrap dress, smoothed it over her hips, then turned away before she could start critiquing her arms or her stomach. The doorbell rang.

"That's gotta be Lisa. Right on cue."

Kayla opened the door to a burst of perfume, cold air, and attitude.

"Bitch, it smells like heaven in here," Lisa announced, strutting in with a bottle of red wine held high like a trophy. Her fiery hair was twisted into a messy bun that somehow looked intentional, her fitted blazer over skinny jeans giving "I close deals and break hearts" simultaneously.

"Don't come in here cussing at my door," Kayla laughed, leaning in for a hug. "Give me this." She took the wine, checking the label. "You went fancy tonight."

"I got a bonus. Let me show off," Lisa replied, already toeing off her heels. "Where my girls at?"

"Early bird gets the macaroni bubbles," Kayla said, heading back to the kitchen.

Lisa followed, perching on one of the barstools. "You look cute, Kay. I like this dress."

"You only saying that 'cause you know I cooked."

"Both can be true," Lisa shrugged.

The door opened again without a knock.

"Y'all better not be talking about me," Jasmine called out, stepping in with a grocery store cake balanced in one hand. She was in scrubs, hair wrapped in a colorful scarf, sneakers looking like they'd seen a twelve-hour shift.

"Hey, mama!" Kayla greeted, crossing the room to hug her.

Jasmine melted into the hug for a second before rolling her eyes up at the ceiling. "If one more grown man comes in my office crying about performance reviews I'ma start charging for therapy," she said, kicking the door shut behind her.

"HR Jesus," Lisa said, making the sign of the cross. "Bless 'em and block 'em."

They all laughed.

"Where's Sarah?" Jasmine asked, dropping the cake on the counter. "She's usually here with a spreadsheet and a salad, judging us."

Kayla smirked. "She said she's coming straight from work. Probably had a date with Excel."

"Or with that lame accountant she keeps pretending she's not dating," Lisa added. "Girl swears she doesn't like him but stays letting him fix her taxes."

Kayla's phone buzzed on the counter.

Sarah: Parking. Save me wings.

Kayla typed back a chicken emoji and a side-eye face.

Michelle was last, like always—bursting in with her giant tote bag, paint on her hands, and some wild new hair color. Tonight it was turquoise tips fading into her curls like the ocean.

"I brought cookies!" she announced. "And by brought I mean I stopped at that bakery y'all like and lied like I made them."

"Long as they sugar and butter, I don't care if they fell from the sky," Jasmine said.

By the time they were all gathered, it was the same old ritual: plates piled high, wine poured, shoes off, legs tucked under them on Kayla's big sectional.

From the outside looking in, they were four polished women and one very intentional hostess. Anyone passing by the window would see a group of successful friends having a lovely evening. Nobody would see the stories that got them there.

They met ten years earlier, long before the Sunday feasts and inside jokes, in a sterile conference basement with stale coffee and bad lighting.

Back then, Kayla had been sitting in a corner at a professional development seminar, tugging at the hem of a blazer that wouldn't quite button. The chairs were too small, the room too cold, and the presenter too boring. "Networking Breakfast for Young Professionals," the flyer had said. In reality, it was a room full of people pretending not to be awkward.

She remembered how alone she had felt that day. Too big for the chairs, too quiet for the loud talkers, too... extra whenever she laughed. She was scrolling mindlessly through her phone to avoid eye contact when a chair scraped beside her.

"You look like you're making a grocery list to survive this," a voice said.

Kayla looked up to see Lisa—back then with a sharp bob, red lipstick, and the kind of confidence that made people look twice.

"I'm counting exits," Kayla confessed. "In case I need to fake a bathroom break and never come back."

Lisa laughed, tipping her head back. "I like you already. I'm Lisa." She stuck out her hand.

"Kayla."

"Well, Kayla, if we suffer, we suffer together."

They'd spent the rest of the session whispering sarcastic commentary and grading everyone's outfits. When the seminar ended, Lisa had said: "I'm not done complaining. Want to get brunch?" Kayla had hesitated, then surprised herself by saying yes.

That brunch turned into a three-hour conversation and the first of many shared plates.

A year later, it was Lisa who dragged Kayla to a charity mixer downtown.

"I don't belong here," Kayla had said, smoothing her thrift-store dress while other women floated by in designer gowns.

"You belong anywhere I say you belong," Lisa replied, taking her hand. "Now stand up straight. If anybody asks, we own the building."

They ended up stuck at a high-top with no chairs. Kayla's feet hurt in the cheap heels she was still breaking in. That's when a woman with curls pinned back and a name tag that read Jasmine – HR Manager approached, holding two glasses of wine and an expression that said she'd rather be home.

"Some guy just told me I 'look like I'm good with people' and tried to hand me his resume," Jasmine muttered, accidently joining their circle. "If I see one more LinkedIn pitch—sorry, I'm talking too much."

"You're in HR?" Lisa asked, eyes lighting up. "You must have stories."

Jasmine gave them a sly smile. "You have no idea."

She told them about the time a manager asked if she could "write up" someone for having bad vibes. Kayla laughed so hard she almost dropped her drink.

"You here alone?" Kayla asked when she caught her breath.

"Girl, yes. My cousin bailed. I don't know anybody here."

"You do now," Lisa said, hooking an arm through Jasmine's. "We're forming a support group."

"Survivors of Awkward Events," Kayla added.

"Wine included," Jasmine said.

By the end of the night, they'd swapped numbers and promises to hang out somewhere that didn't require name tags.

Sarah came next.

It was one of those free Thursday night finance workshops at the community center. Kayla had gone because she kept telling herself "next year I'm gonna get my money right," and this time she meant it. She'd shown up late, slid into a seat, and tried to look like she understood compound interest.

During the Q&A, a woman in a sleek navy dress raised her hand and politely dismantled the presenter's entire example with better math and better charts.

"Okay, Miss Wall Street," someone behind Kayla mumbled.

Afterward, Kayla lingered over the handouts, pretending to read while she silently panicked over her credit card balance. The navy-dress woman approached.

"You look like you're about to try to memorize this whole packet," she said.

Kayla chuckled. "I'm about to frame it and pray over it."

"I'm Sarah," she said, adjusting her glasses. "You want help making a basic budget? I do this for fun."

"Budget for fun? You okay?" Kayla asked.

Sarah actually laughed. "I like order. It calms me down. And I like seeing women know what their money's doing."

Kayla hesitated, then handed over her crumpled worksheet. Sarah studied it, asked a few questions, then started scribbling.

"Alright, here's your next month," she said. "If you follow this, you'll still be broke, but at least you'll know why."

Kayla laughed again, brighter this time. "Can I pay you?"

"For this? No. Just… don't ghost me if I text you about your grocery receipts."

Kayla didn't ghost her. She introduced her to Lisa and Jasmine at the next brunch. By the end of the meal, Sarah was saying things like, "Okay, if you guys insist on buying brunch every week, at least let me move money from your 'bad decisions' fund."

Michelle was the wild card.

Kayla met her on a rainy Saturday at a pop-up art fair. She had gone alone after the girls bailed—Lisa for a date, Jasmine for a family thing, Sarah for a deadline. Kayla had wandered between booths, pretending she was the kind of woman who collected art instead of dishes from Target.

One canvas stopped her cold.

It was a plus-size Black woman on a beach, laughing with her head thrown back, hair wild in the wind. Her stomach was visible, soft and unhidden, and she looked… happy. Whole.

It made Kayla's throat tighten.

"You like her?" a voice said.

Kayla turned. The artist—Michelle—was sitting cross-legged on a stool, purple paint streaked across her forearm, curls tucked under a beanie.

"She's beautiful," Kayla said. "I don't really see… us… like this. On walls."

"That's why I paint her," Michelle replied. "Women come by, look at her, then hide their stomachs like I caught them naked." She shook her head. "I'm like, sis, you look closer to God like that."

Kayla laughed, surprised at how quickly it came.

Michelle watched her for a second. "You want to hold her?" she asked, nodding at the canvas.

Kayla blinked. "For real?"

"Yeah. She's not fragile. Neither are you."

Kayla held the painting, feeling ridiculous and emotional at the same time. Something hot pricked behind her eyes.

"How much is she?" Kayla asked softly.

Michelle named a price. Not cheap, not outrageous. Kayla thought of her budget, of Sarah's little charts and "future you will thank me."

Then she thought of all the times she'd stood in front of her own mirror, sucking in her stomach, avoiding her own eyes.

"I'll take her," Kayla said.

"Good. I want her to live somewhere she's appreciated," Michelle smiled. "I'm Michelle, by the way."

"Kayla."

They got coffee right there in the rain, huddled under one umbrella while Michelle explained her love for color and bodies and chaos. When Kayla introduced her to the group at the next Feast and Talk, Michelle walked into the condo, spotted the painting on Kayla's wall, and said, "Oh yeah. She's home."

Back on the couch now, years later, the five of them had settled into their usual positions: Lisa with a glass of wine cradled in her palm, Jasmine curled up with a throw blanket, Sarah with a small notebook tucked beside her "just in case," Michelle half-sitting, half-lying sideways, her feet in Kayla's lap.

"Okay, story time," Lisa announced. "Kayla, this lasagna—"

"It's shrimp and grits, white girl," Jasmine cut in.

"Whatever. It's doing things to my soul. You cooked like somebody's uncle just came home from jail."

They all cackled.

"Thank you... I think?" Kayla said.

"So," Lisa continued, "who's gonna admit they did something dumb for a man this week? I'll start. I drove forty minutes out my way to 'accidentally' run into Darren at that bar he likes. This man didn't even show up. I played myself."

"Again?" Sarah asked, eyebrows raised.

"Don't do that, spreadsheet," Lisa warned. "Judgment is how wrinkles are born."

"You don't need my judgment," Sarah replied. "You need standards."

"I have standards," Lisa protested. "He just doesn't meet them yet."

"Oooh, girl," Michelle said, shaking her head. "Put that on a pillow."

"Oh, like you don't have a story," Jasmine chimed in. "Didn't you let Tyler move in for 'two weeks' and now it's been six months and he's rearranging your furniture?"

"That man vacuumed," Michelle said defensively. "With intention. Do you know how rare that is?"

"With your vacuum," Sarah muttered.

They all laughed, even Michelle.

Jasmine sighed. "At least y'all got furniture-moving problems. My situation can't even commit to a text thread."

"That situationship still alive?" Lisa asked.

"Girl, I don't even know. He's good with the late-night calls, and the 'I miss you' speeches…Then disappears when I mention brunch in the daylight. I'm too old for this."

"You are," Sarah said plainly.

"Thank you, calendar," Jasmine shot back.

They dissolved into laughter again. The jokes bounced around Kayla, and she laughed too, timed just right so nobody noticed that most of the stories started the same way: my man, this guy I'm seeing, the dude I'm talking to.

When eyes finally turned to her, it was Jasmine who asked the question gently.

"What about you, Kay? Any contenders?"

Kayla took a slow sip of her drink, stared into the glass like the answer might be floating in there.

"Nah," she said lightly. "You know me. I just flirt with my skincare bottles and go to bed early."

Lisa rolled her eyes. "Girl, you be hiding. Every time we out, men be looking and you got your head in your phone."

"They not looking at me," Kayla said, trying to keep her tone playful.

"They are," Michelle insisted. "You just don't let 'em."

Kayla shrugged, her smile stretched tight. "I'm good. I got y'all. I got my business. I'm happy."

On the surface, it sounded convincing. They nodded, let it go, moved on to gossip about coworkers and vacations and Michelle's latest art commission.

Kayla refilled everyone's glasses, topping off her own last. The conversation flowed over her like warm water. She tossed in comments here and there, made jokes, refilled bowls, played the role she knew by heart: the funny, dependable friend. The one who hosted, who listened, who clapped when the others told stories about roses showing up at their jobs, surprise weekend trips, random "thinking about you" cash apps.

Nobody asked her when was the last time somebody looked at her like that painting on the wall.

Later that night, after everyone had gone home and Kayla had stacked dishes in the sink, the condo fell silent. The kind of silence that presses against your chest.

She stood in front of that same full-length mirror, barefoot now, makeup smudged, dress slightly wrinkled. She'd just sent the "text me when you get home" messages and gotten the "home safe, love you" replies.

She stared at her reflection. The same one that had smiled and laughed and brushed men off in the stories her friends told.

In the dim light, without the noise, she saw other things: the way her arms pushed against the sleeves, the curve of her stomach beneath the fabric, the slight sag of her shoulders when she wasn't holding them up for anyone else.

For a moment, she let her smile drop.

"You're fine," she told herself out loud. "You're successful. You got friends. You're building something. You're fine."

A part of her believed it. Another part of her—smaller but louder tonight—whispered back: Then why do you feel so alone?

She thought about Lisa's loud stories, Jasmine's tired jokes, Sarah's calm certainty, Michelle's playful chaos. All of them had their mess, their heartbreaks, their foolish men.

But they also had something she didn't have, that special someone. Even if he was the wrong someone, inconsistency wrapped in good perfume. There was at least a text to overanalyze, a name to curse, a chest to lay a head on, even if it wasn't permanent.

Kayla had… her phone, her mirror, and an extra plate of food she pretended she'd made "just in case somebody dropped by." Nobody ever did.

Her stomach growled. She laughed a little at herself, shook off the heaviness, and went to the kitchen. Maybe she ate more than she needed to. Maybe she moved around the condo cleaning things that were already clean. Maybe she lingered too long on the couch scrolling through social media, double-tapping engagement photos and baby showers and anniversary dinners until her chest felt tight.

Eventually, she turned off the TV. The glow from the painting in the living room caught her eye again—the laughing woman on the beach, soft and unapologetic.

Kayla walked over and touched the bottom edge of the frame.

"I'm gonna catch up to you one day," she said quietly.

Then she turned off the light and went to bed.

4

LINES WE DON'T CROSS

For Kayla, Monday began with the biting kind of cold Chicago reserved for people who didn't want to leave their beds. She stepped out of the Uber with her coffee cupped between both hands, holding it against her chest like it was the last warm thing on earth. Her heels tapped against the concrete as she hurried inside the steel and-glass building that towered over the street like a monument to stress.

The lobby smelled like citrus polish and ambition. People moved with purpose, eyes focused, and voices low. Kayla slipped into the elevator and pressed the button to her floor, already bracing herself for the day. She didn't hate her job, not exactly. She hated being invisible inside of it. She was the one they called when everything fell apart, but never the one they called into the room where decisions were made.

When she reached her desk, her inbox was already bleeding with red "urgent" flags.

I need those numbers revised before 10.

Follow up with accounting ASAP.

Also, schedule me a haircut.

Kayla stared at that last one, blinked twice, and whispered under her breath, "You grown-ass man... book your own haircut." She dropped her bag and powered on her computer, willing herself not to flip the desk.

Her coworker, Janelle, walked in like the building was hers, wearing a camel blazer, sleek bun, and the effortless glow of someone who actually slept at night. She perched on the corner of Kayla's desk.

"You look like you're about to quit," Janelle said.

"I wanted to quit last year," Kayla replied dryly. "Today is just the sequel."

"What ridiculous task is he sending you now? Heart transplant? Brain surgery?"

"Worse," Kayla said. "He wants me to schedule his haircut."

Janelle shook her head slowly. "I pray for you. Daily."

Kayla's phone buzzed. A message from Michelle.

Don't forget we're meeting Jasmine tonight. She has 'news.'

Kayla texted back, God. She's not pregnant, is she?

Michelle replied instantly. No. If she was, she'd send us a calendar invite.

Kayla laughed out loud, loud enough to get side-eyes from two desks away. It felt good, even for a second, to let something break through the monotony.

The rest of the day blurred into emails, phone calls, follow-ups, and moments where Kayla had to physically remind herself not to curse her boss out. By mid-afternoon her brain felt mushy, her patience thin, her spirit craving escape. When the clock finally hit quitting time, she packed quickly and headed to the garage.

The silence inside her car felt holy.

She needed this night with her girls.

Jasmine's condo sat high above the city, all clean lines, white walls, and a subtle smell of expensive candles. Kayla knocked once, and Michelle's laughter poured through the door before it even opened.

Jasmine swung it wide staring at Kayla. "Finally. We were literally starting to talk shit."

"You talk shit when I'm here," Kayla said, stepping inside.

"And we do it very well," Michelle added, curled up on the couch, shoes already off and a bowl of popcorn in her lap like it was her natural habitat.

Jasmine poured wine for all of them—red for herself, white for Michelle, and rosé for Kayla. They had their styles, their flavors, and never had to ask. That was the beauty of their circle: they understood each other without explanation.

"Okay," Jasmine said, settling into her chair with her legs crossed. "Let's get to it."

Michelle pointed at her with her bowl. "Yes. Because you texted us with urgency. I had to stop watching my show."

Jasmine inhaled, sat straighter, and said, "I got offered a promotion."

Kayla's mouth fell open. "Jasmine! That's incredible!"

Michelle clapped loudly. "Look at you! Climbing ladders!"

"Wait," Jasmine said, raising her hand. "Before you start planning a celebration… the job is in London."

The entire room stilled.

Kayla blinked. "London as in… the actual London?"

"Yes," Jasmine said. "As in tea, royalty, and men with accents that make you irresponsible."

Michelle leaned forward. "For how long?"

"Two years."

Kayla felt something sink inside her. Not sharply, not painfully. Just a slow, quiet drop—like the floor shifting an inch beneath her feet.

Michelle was the heart.

Jasmine was the anchor.

Kayla was the one always trying to stand in the middle and balance the weight of both.

"What are you thinking?" Kayla asked softly.

Jasmine stared down at her wine. "I'm thinking… it's everything I've worked for. Everything I've wanted. But it means leaving you two. It means leaving home."

Michelle scooted closer. "You're not leaving us, Jasmine. You're expanding. We'll visit. You'll be back. We're not going anywhere."

Kayla nodded. "You'll FaceTime us every morning. We both know you will."

Jasmine cracked a tiny smile. "I would."

"But be honest," Michelle said gently. "You already made your decision. You just needed to hear us say it's okay."

Jasmine lowered her eyes. It was true.

Kayla reached out and touched her knee. "We are proud of you. We always will be. Even if you move across the world."

Jasmine blinked fast—her version of being emotional. "You two are my family," she whispered. "My real family."

"And you'll still have us," Michelle said. "Just with a six-hour time difference."

Kayla forced a laugh. "London men iron their clothes. That alone is worth going for."

Jasmine laughed through her tears. "Facts."

How much time do we have left," Kayla asked.

"Yeah! When do we say Bon Voyage? Michelle added.

"Three months," Jasmine answered.

"Three months! That's a life time for some people," Kayla said.

"I know what we can all do before you leave us. Let's plan a trip," Michelle suggested.

"That sounds like a great idea!" Jasmine acknowledges.

But as the night softened into familiar chatter, second glasses of wine, and the comfortable ache of long friendship, Kayla felt something tighten inside her.

A quiet fear.

A small loneliness.

A question she didn't want to face yet.

If Jasmine left…

If Michelle's life kept moving faster…

If Marcus never called again…

Where did that leave her?

Later, as she sipped her rosé and stared out at the glittering city through Jasmine's windows, she felt the truth settle gently but firmly inside her.

There was a fine line between being independent and being lonely.

And Kayla was beginning to realize she was standing right on it.

5

WINE, WORK, AND THE WEIGHT OF SECRETS

Thursday nights belonged to the girls. No matter how long their week had been or how many responsibilities tugged at them from every direction, Thursdays stayed untouched. It wasn't just tradition anymore; it was survival. It was the one place they didn't have to perform strength or patience or charm. Just themselves.

Kayla arrived last—not out of lateness, but preference. She liked the moment she walked in and saw them all looking her way. It reminded her she belonged somewhere, even if the world outside didn't always make her feel that way.

Venessa was glowing that night, the way it always did. The wine lounge lived in a narrow alley between a gallery and a florist that smelled permanently of rain. Inside, soft amber lighting brushed every table, warming faces and softening edges. It was an easy place to breathe, a place that made everyone look a little better than they felt.

The girls were already tucked into their booth when Kayla walked in.

Lisa spotted her first. She waved dramatically, bracelets jangling. "Kayla! Finally. We were two seconds from filing a missing person's report."

Jasmine, always gentle, smiled up at her. "Come sit, sweetheart. You look beautiful tonight."

Michelle leaned forward, studying Kayla's hair. "What did you do? This is giving 'quiet luxury' and I love it for you."

Kayla slid into the booth and adjusted her plum dress. "I didn't do anything special. Humidity is just flirting with me today."

Sarah eyed her with warm approval. "Well, it's working. You look gorgeous."

Kayla accepted the compliments with a smile she had learned to make look effortless. Inside, they landed in the more tender parts of her—the places that were still learning to believe them.

Their server approached with the familiarity of someone who'd seen their chaos before. "Ladies, the usual wine flight?"

Lisa said, "Absolutely. And bring the truffle flatbread before Kayla starts pretending, she doesn't eat carbs."

Kayla narrowed her eyes. "I don't pretend anything. I have standards."

Michelle grinned. "Standards until someone brings out challah bread."

Their laughter rolled across the table, rich and loud, uncaring of who heard it.

When the drinks arrived, conversation turned naturally toward work.

Sarah was the first to dive in. "If one more junior analyst hands me numbers that don't add up, I swear I'm filing a complaint with whoever runs finance heaven. Or hell. Doesn't matter."

Lisa rested her chin on her palm. "You need a vacation. Somewhere men don't say EBITDA like its foreplay."

Michelle perked up. "Speaking of vacations… I'm thinking Greece this summer. Santorini. Mykonos. I want blue rooftops and questionable decisions."

Jasmine nodded vigorously. "Yes. Something far away from men who think discrimination law is optional reading."

Kayla listened as they joked and vented and sipped their wine.

They were loud, brilliant women with big voices and even bigger spirits. Being around them always reminded Kayla of who she wanted to be, a person that was stronger, louder, more certain of herself.

But then, as always, the topic shifted.

Lisa tapped her glass. "Dating updates. Who's entertaining someone new?"

Michelle raised her hand. "Me. I met someone in Austin last week."

Sarah groaned. "Not another creative poet who journals under the moon."

"A structural engineer," Michelle said smugly. "He journals about bridges."

The table burst into laughter.

Then the attention turned, naturally and almost too quickly, to Kayla.

"Well?" Jasmine asked softly. "Anything new?"

Kayla shrugged. "Not really. Work has been taking all my time."

Lisa reached over and squeezed her hand. "Just remember, you deserve a man who actually sees you."

"I'm not forcing anything," Kayla said, her voice even but a little thin at the edges.

Sarah nodded. "Good. The wrong man is a liability. And you don't have space for liabilities."

Kayla smiled, but something in her chest tightened. Not from offense, not from sadness—just a quiet, familiar ache. She wanted to believe she radiated the strength her friends saw in her. She wanted to believe she wasn't invisible in rooms where others shined. She wanted to believe she didn't long for someone to choose her.

Michelle watched her carefully. "Can I say something without making you sad?"

Kayla tilted her head. "That depends."

"Men notice you," Michelle said. "More than you realize. You have this… quiet power."

Jasmine nodded, firm in her tone. "It's true. In HR, I can always tell when men pay attention. They pay attention to you."

Kayla offered a soft smile, but inside, she didn't quite buy it. Her insecurities whispered louder than their reassurances.

When the flatbread and small plates arrived, the conversation blossomed again—stories, complaints, jokes.

Lisa told them about the man who called himself a "financial visionary" while still living with his mother and trading crypto from her basement.

Sarah almost choked on her drink. "That's not finance. That's advanced gambling."

Michelle wiped tears of laughter. "Did he at least have a haircut?"

Lisa scoffed. "Not a single fade in sight."

Kayla laughed until her shoulders shook, and for a little while the weight inside her loosened.

By the time they paid the bill, the table was cluttered with empty glasses and plates, evidence of a night spent spilling honesty and joy in equal measure.

Outside, the valet pulled up their cars. One by one, the girls hugged her tightly—warm, real, grounding.

"Text us when you get home," Jasmine said.

"Love you, babe," Lisa added.

"Same time next week," Michelle reminded.

Kayla nodded and slipped into her car. The interior smelled like her perfume, her lotion, faint traces of her day. It was quiet, warm, safe.

But the drive home stripped away the laughter and dimmed the glow of the wine. In the dark, her reflection in the window looked softer, more honest. She wondered, not for the first time, why love always seemed to pass her by. Why she could be celebrated by her friends yet overlooked everywhere else. Why she felt almost chosen but never truly claimed.

Her eyes misted, just slightly, but she wiped them before tears could fall. She refused to cry here, in the quiet of her car, with the city buzzing around her.

Not tonight.

Not yet.

She would save that for a moment, in some quiet corner all to herself, where no one could hear her break.

6

BARCELONA NIGHTS

The airport buzzed with the kind of bright, restless energy only a girls' trip could produce. Kayla stood beside her oversized mint-green suitcase, packed with outfits she hoped would make her feel as confident as her friends already looked. Lisa had insisted they coordinate travel outfits, so the five of them now stood in a row like a glamorous, slightly disorganized fashion ad.

Lisa, sharp in cream trousers and a silk blouse, flicked her fiery red hair with theatrical confidence.

"Barcelona is not ready for us," she announced, loud enough to turn a few heads.

Jasmine adjusted her gold-rimmed glasses and exhaled.

"Speak for yourself. HR drained my soul. I might sleep for the entire first half of this trip."

Sarah pressed their boarding passes tightly together like she was corralling children.

"Let's just get to the gate on time. Every time we travel, one of you wanders off."

Michelle, radiant in a bright patterned jumpsuit, threw her arms in the air.

"Ladies, I am officially on vacation. I'm eating everything, drinking everything, and dancing on anything that doesn't move."

The group burst into laughter.

Kayla laughed too—quiet, small, measured. She adored these women. They made her feel grounded, seen, included. But beneath the warmth, a whisper lingered in the private corners of her mind:

You're the odd one out.

The one man overlook.

The one who blends into the background.

She forced the thought away and boarded the plane with the rest of them.

BARCELONA FELT like stepping into a living postcard, vivid blue skies, warm breezes, streets packed with life. The scent of sea salt and roasted almonds followed them all the way to their hotel overlooking La Barceloneta Beach.

The moment their luggage hit the floor; the girls were already changing into swimsuits.

Lisa was first onto the balcony, gripping the railing as she stared out at the panoramic sweep of umbrellas and shimmering waves.

"Oh my God. This is it. This is luxury. This is wealth."

Michelle called from inside, full of drama.

"Someone help me with sunscreen! I absolutely refuse to crisp like a croissant."

Kayla adjusted her black one-piece carefully in the mirror. It hugged her curves in a way that made her both proud and self-conscious. She tied her sarong, retied it, adjusted it again, hoping it looked intentional rather than anxious.

Jasmine appeared behind her reflection, smiling softly.

"You look stunning, Kay."

Kayla held the smile, but the flicker of doubt in her eyes gave her away for half a second. Jasmine noticed; she always did.

. . .

THE BEACH BAR was alive with music drifting on the wind, laughter from men who'd already had too much sangria, and the shuffle of waiters carrying cocktails with fruit spears.

The moment the girls approached; attention hit them like a wave.

Italian tourists surrounded Lisa and Michelle almost instantly.

"Bellissima! You join us later, yes?"

"You are too beautiful to sit alone!"

Michelle giggled and twirled, soaking in the attention.

Sarah caught the eye of a handsome British architect who looked like he spent weekends designing skyscrapers and reading poetry.

Three different men offered to carry Jasmine's beach chair before she even sat down.

And Kayla?

A polite smile from a waiter.

Nothing more.

She sipped her mojito quietly and let the cool mint settle on her tongue. She focused on the water—sunlight glittering over the waves like broken glass. She told herself she didn't care. Told herself invisibility was peaceful.

But her chest tightened anyway.

WHEN THE SUN WENT DOWN, Barcelona transformed. The Gothic Quarter hummed with life—lantern-lit streets, balconies overflowing with flowers, warm air spiced with saffron and sound. The girls wandered through narrow alleys, following the smell of grilled seafood until they reached a tapas bar bright with music and conversation.

Plates arrived in waves, patatas bravas, grilled octopus, garlic and shrimp.

Lisa took a bite of the octopus and moaned dramatically.

"This is better than half the men I've dated."

Michelle clinked her glass.

"To more octopus and fewer disappointments."

Kayla laughed genuinely; the kind of laughter that came from somewhere deeper than amusement. For a brief moment, she felt weightless.

But as they walked to the nightclub in the District of Barcelona, called Eixample, she caught her reflection in a shop window. The neon lights hit her friends like spotlights—sleek, glowing, magazine-ready. Kayla saw her own shape in the glass: thick thighs, soft stomach, full arms. Features she usually embraced now pressed against her with a heaviness she didn't expect.

Inside the club, heat and energy swallowed them. The bass vibrated through the floor, lights sweeping across moving bodies. The place smelled like cologne, sweat, and longing.

Men flocked to her friends instantly.

A tall Brazilian spun Michelle with practiced charm.

Two men fought over who would buy Lisa a drink.

Jasmine and Sarah each had admirers glued to their conversation.

Kayla danced with them, moving her hips to the beat, keeping her smile bright. Dancing made her feel powerful—even when no one watched.

At one point, she noticed a man across the room. Dark curls, warm brown skin, eyes locked on her. Her heart fluttered.

Maybe...

But he walked right past her.

Straight to Lisa.

Something inside Kayla cracked—not loudly, not visibly, but in a way, she felt deep in her ribs. She kept dancing, but the joy had slipped through her fingers.

EVENTUALLY SHE SLIPPED OUT to the rooftop terrace of the club. Barcelona stretched before her—lights scattered like fallen stars, the night pulsing with energy she couldn't quite claim.

She held the railing and breathed, trying to steady herself. The breeze cooled her hot cheeks.

Then the tears came—slow, quiet, patient. Not dramatic. Just truth leaking out after being held in too long.

Why do I always feel like the extra one?

Why am I never the one someone chooses first?

Why am I never enough?

Footsteps approached.

Kayla quickly wiped her face as Jasmine stepped into the light.

"You disappeared," Jasmine said gently. "Talk to me."

"I JUST NEEDED AIR," Kayla whispered.

Jasmine studied her, seeing through the lie.

"Kayla… don't do that. Not with me."

The softness in her voice broke through Kayla's last layer of restraint.

"Sometimes I feel like I'm watching everyone else live," Kayla said quietly. "Like I'm there, but not really part of anything. Like I don't… matter the same way."

Jasmine stepped closer, placing a warm hand on her shoulder.

"You listen to me. You are beautiful. You are smart. You are loved. God did not put you here to blend into the background."

Kayla's eyes shimmered again.

"Then why do I feel invisible?"

"Because the wrong people are looking," Jasmine whispered. "Your person will see you. I promise."

Kayla folded into her arms, letting her friend's strength hold her up. When she pulled away, she wiped her cheeks, reapplied her lip gloss, and straightened her dress.

Mask back on.

She returned to the dance floor, laughing when Michelle nearly toppled off the DJ booth, letting the rhythm pull her back into the moment. But she carried the rooftop quiet inside her, tucked beneath her smile.

BY THE TIME the girls stumbled back to their hotel—heels dangling from their fingers, hair messy, laughter echoing down the hallway—

Barcelona was already easing into sunrise.

Kayla laughed with them, warm and breathless.

But when the lights went out and the others drifted into sleep, she slipped onto the balcony alone. The pink horizon stretched before her, and the city hummed a soft lullaby.

She let the breeze cradle her sadness until her breath steadied...

Then she slipped back into bed until sleep finally carried her away.

7

TRYING TO BE ENOUGH

Barcelona feeling heavier than when she left. Sunlight and wine and beaches had distracted her, but the moment she stepped back into her Chicago apartment, the same old quite wrapped around her like a familiar coat. She unpacked slowly, letting the silence swallow the last bits of vacation glow.

One morning before work, she stood in front of the mirror, staring at herself with a tired honesty. Same curls. Same cheeks. Same curves. She touched her face gently, trying to see something new there.

"Come on, Kay," she whispered. "Get it together."

She didn't dislike herself. She just didn't feel like she ever changed, even when she tried.

So, she tried harder.

She bought new clothes, nicer ones, pieces that felt more expensive against her skin. She studied makeup tutorials and practiced blending foundation until her arm hurt. She switched her perfume to something warmer, something that promised confidence in its description. She began waking up earlier for morning walks, blending smoothies, writing short affirmations she barely believed.

But every night, after she undressed and washed her face, she felt exactly the same.

Still invisible.

Still overlooked.

Still... Kayla.

One night, sitting on her couch with a blanket wrapped around her legs, she downloaded three dating apps in a row. She filled out her profiles carefully, picking photos that made her look bright and comfortable, describing herself in a way she hoped didn't sound forced.

The messages came quickly.

The first man opened with "Hey gorgeous ."

She ignored him.

The second asked her if she wanted to "link tonight."

Blocked.

The third seemed promising. They talked for a week. He asked thoughtful questions. Then he disappeared. No explanation.

Another almost.

The fourth man took her out for coffee. He smiled at her in a polite, nervous way. Their conversation was fine. Not amazing, not terrible. But halfway through the date, he said, "You're prettier in person. Honestly, I was worried."

She finished the date, smiled through it, and never responded to him again.

Another almost.

The fifth man was the one she liked. They talked every morning and every night for nearly three weeks. She laughed at his jokes, reread their messages, let her heart open just a little. She imagined what their first date might be like.

Then he sent the message that broke the spell completely:

"You're amazing, but I'm not ready for something serious."

Kayla stared at the words for a long moment, then placed her phone face down on her chest. She didn't cry. She didn't yell. She just lay there feeling emptied.

"I'm trying," she whispered into the quiet room. "I really am."

But she kept going anyway. She kept styling her hair. Kept doing her makeup. Kept dressing in outfits she hoped would pull her forward into a different version of herself. She wanted to be seen. Really seen. Not halfway, not by accident, not as the warming-up act for somebody else's love story.

One evening, after a man from one of the apps asked her for "full body pics," she deleted every app. She closed each one, hit the delete button, and didn't look back.

Afterward, she sat on the floor with her back against the couch and let the quiet settle around her like dust. The city hummed faintly outside her windows.

"I'm tired of trying to be enough," she said softly.

Not dramatic.

Not hysterical.

Just true.

She pulled her knees to her chest and rested her chin against them. She didn't know it, but something in her life was inching closer. Something she couldn't predict or prepare for.

Not love. Not yet.

But the beginning of something.

For now, she closed her eyes and breathed in the stillness, letting herself rest for the first time in weeks.

8

A MAN'S PROWESS ON FULL DISPLAY

Jakil stood in front of the floor-to-ceiling windows of his penthouse, the city spread out below him like a promise, and he let himself stay there longer than necessary, shoulders squared, hands loose at his sides, as if posture alone could hold the weight of everything he'd built. Washington, D.C. glowed in the early evening—headlights inching along the avenues, monuments lit like marble ghosts, glass towers catching the last streaks of sun, the whole city humming with purpose and power. People looked at this view and saw success, a finish line, proof that the grind paid off. He looked at it and saw distance, the measurable space between where he stood and everyone else, the quiet separation that came with being admired more than known.

Behind him, the apartment was quiet. No music, no television, just the faint hum of the building and the occasional ping from his phone lighting up the dark glass. A contract being signed. A seller confirming. A buyer negotiating. Real estate never slept, and neither did the version of himself the city knew: the charismatic broker with the easy smile, the sharp suits, the closing percentage everyone envied. That man existed on autopilot now, a role he stepped into without thinking, like muscle memory. Some days he wondered when it had stopped feeling like ambition and started feeling like obligation.

Every morning, before he became that man, he went to the gym, because discipline made sense there in a way the rest of his life didn't. The day began with the slam of weights, the smell of rubber mats, and the bass of someone's playlist vibrating through the floor. Jakil moved through his sets with practiced focus—bench press, deadlift, pull-ups, rows—counting reps the way some men counted regrets. The gym was the one place where effort equaled results, where the lines on his body matched the discipline in his mind, where no one questioned the equation. He pushed harder than necessary sometimes, chasing the burn because it was honest.

People watched him. Men respected him, nodding in that silent way men did when they recognized work. Women noticed him, eyes lingering just long enough to register interest before looking away. He felt it without needing to look, the same way he felt a room shift when he entered. And later, in conference rooms and luxury condos, clients trusted him. He was their closer. Their fixer. Their "Jak." He knew how to talk numbers, how to talk lifestyle, how to talk them into believing a property could change everything. He sold futures for a living, polished visions wrapped in square footage and light.

But when the day ended and the doors shut behind him, the silence felt louder than the city. It pressed in instead of expanding, filling rooms that looked perfect but felt unfinished.

He had no problem meeting women. That had never been his issue. Attraction came easily, chemistry followed, and connection sparked fast in his orbit. What didn't come easily was staying.

He met Michelle first. They'd crossed paths at a charity gala. He was there to charm the donors, and she was there to protect the organization from lawsuits. Michelle Patel, Indian-American, sharp eyes, sharper tongue, a lawyer who could break down a case and a man in the same sentence. They spent half the night in a corner, arguing about sentencing laws and loopholes in contracts, the kind of argument that felt like foreplay for the mind. She made him think. She made him laugh in a way that surprised him, caught him off guard. He liked that she didn't soften her opinions to make him comfortable.

Later, over dinner at a quiet restaurant, she listened while he talked about his first big sale, about growing up without much and promising himself he'd never go back. She told him about clients who couldn't afford the justice they deserved, about the frustration of knowing the law and watching it fail people anyway. Somewhere between dessert and the bill, he realized he genuinely liked her mind, the way it cut and questioned and didn't flinch.

When they ended up back at his place, the chemistry was real, the connection fast, urgency layered with curiosity.

The moment the door closed behind them; the tension that had simmered all evening surfaced. It wasn't rushed. It was curious. Their kisses were exploratory, like arguments without words—her hands firm at his shoulders, his mouth lingering just long enough to make her inhale sharply before pulling back.

Michelle pressed him lightly, testing him, smiling when he didn't rush her. Jakil liked that she noticed restraint. He guided her with patience, the kind that suggested confidence rather than caution. Every touch felt deliberate, negotiated in silence.

Later, when they lay together, her head resting against his chest, she traced slow, thoughtful lines along his skin, as if memorizing him. He felt it then—that quiet satisfaction that came not from conquest, but from being chosen in the moment.

THE NEXT MORNING WAS EASY. Coffee. Quiet jokes. The soft domestic calm that sometimes tricked him into thinking this was how things could be. She kissed his cheek before she left and told him he surprised her, and the word lingered longer than it should have. He didn't call her for three days. Not out of cruelty, not even intention, but because momentum carried him elsewhere and silence was easier than deciding what he wanted.

By the time he did, something felt dimmed. Not because of anything she'd done, but because the rest of his life roared back in, loud and insistent: Deals, showings, and clients. Michelle could only fit into his spaces and his time, like the margins of his calendar. Eventually, their texts slowed, their dinners faded, and he told himself it was mutual, that adults drifted and that was normal.

Then came Elena. He met her at a rooftop bar during a networking event he'd almost skipped, the kind of night where he considered staying home and then didn't. Elena Ramirez—Latina, founder of a tech startup that was already making noise. She talked with her hands, laughed with her whole body, and had a fire in her eyes that made people move out of her way without realizing they were doing it. She didn't ask what he did until halfway through their conversation, which immediately set her apart.

They spent a night moving from bar to bar, dancing until their clothes clung to their skin, arguing—in the best way—about risk, strategy, and who took bigger bets, founders or brokers. She teased him about playing it too safe. He told her he didn't know how to lose, and she raised an eyebrow like she didn't believe him. The tension between them built slowly and then all at once, sharp and electric.

WITH ELENA, everything ignited faster. Their kiss was heat and challenge, sparked by laughter and sharpened by competition. She pushed him back playfully, then pulled him close just as quickly. Their bodies moved like they were keeping time to a song only they could hear, restless, insistent, alive.

SHE LIKED HIS STRENGTH. He liked her fire. Neither pretended otherwise.

THE NIGHT BURNED hot and bright, fueled by adrenaline and mutual hunger. Her hands slid around his waist, fingers hooking with confidence, pulling him in until her laughter brushed his lips. She kissed him like she challenged him—mouth firm, teeth grazing, heat rising fast. Jakil responded instinctively, hands finding her hips, thumbs pressing into the curve as she arched closer.

She loved the contrast—the hard planes of his body against her movement, the way his neck flexed when she tugged him closer. Her lips traced the line of his jaw, lingered at his ear, breath warm and teasing.

The night unfolded in momentum—bodies colliding, separating, returning. When it slowed, they lay side by side, shoulders touching, skin still humming. He felt the thrill of intensity—but also its limit.

And when it was over, they lay side by side, breathing hard, staring at the ceiling like runners after a race, satisfied, spent, already thinking about what came next.

THE MORNING AFTER, she stretched in his bed and checked her email before she even looked at him. He watched her smile at a message from one of her investors and realized she was already halfway gone, mentally back in her world. He respected that. He also understood it, maybe too well. They tried for a while. Late-night calls. Quick dinners between her flights and his closings. But their ambition lived louder than their feelings, and neither of them was willing to turn the volume down. Eventually, they stopped trying to harmonize.

OLIVIA ARRIVED LIKE A PAINTING. He met her at an art gallery opening, the kind of event where people pretended to care more about the work than who else was there. Olivia Mitchell, African-American, art curator, elegant in a black dress that draped like water, moved through the room like she belonged to the walls themselves. She spoke about artists the way some people spoke about gods, reverent but critical, unafraid to name flaws.

He stood beside her in front of a piece made of broken glass and metal, and she said, "People will say this is about destruction, but it's not. It's about survival." The statement landed somewhere unexpected in him. He asked her questions he wouldn't have asked anyone else, questions that weren't about outcome but meaning. She answered like she wasn't rushing to impress him, like time bent around her when she spoke. Later, they walked through the city, talking about representation in museums, about how art could shift culture slowly, quietly, permanently.

Dinner turned into a nightcap. The nightcap turned into something deeper, softer, heavier than he anticipated.

OLIVIA UNFOLDED SLOWLY. Their intimacy felt like art—measured, intentional, layered with meaning. She studied him even as she touched him, her fingers tracing lines the way she might trace brushstrokes, lingering where the story felt richest. Her nails followed the ink on his arm, then slipped beneath, exploring muscle as if mapping history. She kissed him softly at first, lips barely there, then deeper—measured, unhurried. Jakil felt himself slow, matching her cadence, aware of every point of contact.

She rested her forehead against his collarbone, breath warm against his skin, and he felt the intimacy of that small space—the hollow at her throat, the gentle rise and fall of her chest beneath his hand.

WHEN THEY FINALLY CAME TOGETHER, it felt less like urgency and more like surrender—to the moment, to the quiet understanding between them.

Afterward, she lay against him, her hand resting over his heart, as if listening for something unspoken. He felt seen in a way that unsettled him.

AT DAYBREAK, she traced the tattoos on his arm and told him his body told stories even before he opened his mouth. He almost told her something real in return, something unguarded. Almost. But then came another gallery opening. Another donor dinner. Another property showing. Their lives ran parallel—beautiful, accomplished, busy, but their lines didn't touch, no matter how close they ran.

ISABELLA WAS DIFFERENT. He met her in New York on a quick trip for a client who wanted a pied-à-terre near Central Park. She was Italian, a fashion designer consulting for a luxury brand. They collided—literally—in a hotel lobby, her fabric samples flying everywhere like spilled color. He knelt to help, and somehow an apology turned into espresso, which turned into a slow stroll through streets lit by store windows and taxicab lights.

Isabella saw the world in color and shape. She tugged at his collar, critiqued his suit, and told him how she'd redesign the lines, how structure could still be sensual. He'd never cared about stitching or drape before, but listening to her, he did. When he extended his trip for one more night, he didn't pretend it was just for business.

ISABELLA BROUGHT TEXTURE TO EVERYTHING. She tugged at his shirt, adjusting his collar, tugged lightly at his sleeve, her fingers grazing wrist, forearm, shoulder—always assessing, always smiling. Her kiss came suddenly, playful but precise, lips soft, then demanding, as if she'd decided exactly how it should feel. laughing softly as she critiqued the way it fit him, her fingers already imagining something better. Her kisses were playful, her movements fluid, like she was arranging a scene rather than rushing through it.

Jakil let her lead, intrigued by the way she shaped the moment—pulling him closer, then stepping back to look at him, as if assessing a design. When she finally settled against him, it felt intentional, curated, perfect in its imperfection. Jakil's hands found the small of her back, tracing the elegant line of her spine. She hummed quietly at the contact, pressing closer, her mouth warm at his neck, teeth grazing just enough to leave him aware of every nerve.

. . .

THE FOLLOWING DAY, she sketched him while he pretended not to notice, the scratch of pencil soft and steady. When he finally looked, she'd captured something gentler in his face than he'd ever seen in the mirror. He kept the sketch, and told himself it was because it was good art. He knew better, and the knowing sat with him longer than the goodbye.

And then there was Aisha. He met her at a lecture, he only attended, because a client gave him the ticket. Aisha Khan, Pakistani-American, scientist, brilliant enough to make half the room look like they were in the wrong building. She spoke about dark matter and the future of space research, and he sat there wondering how anyone could make physics sound like poetry. He waited for her afterward, half convinced he was out of his depth. She laughed when he told her that.

"So?" she said. "Curiosity is enough."

They met for coffee. Then dinner. Then more. Their conversations were long, winding things that left his mind buzzing, the kind that made him look at the world slightly differently afterward. They didn't agree on everything. They didn't have to. One thing led to another in its own time, unforced, patient.

WITH AISHA, everything slowed—unnervingly so.

She stood close without touching him at first, her presence alone shifting the air. When she finally reached for him, her fingers slid gently along his forearm, not testing strength but acknowledging it. Jakil felt himself exhale before he realized he'd been holding his breath.

Their kiss was quiet. Deep. Her lips lingered, unhurried, as if time had widened around them. She rested her forehead against his, nose brushing his cheek, breath syncing with his. When her hand slipped to the back of his neck, her thumb traced a slow, grounding line that sent a shiver through him.

Jakil pulled her closer, one hand settling at her waist, feeling the warmth there, the way her body fit against his without effort. She rested her ear against his chest, listening, smiling softly.

Later, she lay beside him, fingers idly tracing constellations along his shoulder, her voice low as she spoke about stars, distance, possibility. Jakil stared at the ceiling, chest full in a way that unsettled him.

For the first time, the silence didn't feel empty.

It felt dangerous.

AT THE BREAK OF DAWN, she lay with her head on his chest, telling him about a future mission she hoped to be part of, about places beyond the atmosphere and questions humanity hadn't answered yet. She spoke like the sky wasn't the limit, just the starting point. He felt small in the best way, grounded and unsettled all at once.

And yet.

Each of these women impressed him. Each connection lit something. They weren't forgettable. They weren't interchangeable. They stayed with him in fragments, in memory flashes, in quiet moments. But none of it lasted. Not because they weren't enough—but because he wasn't willing to be present where things asked for more than moments.

Jakil stared at his reflection in the dark glass of his penthouse windows later that night. The city glittered behind him, vast and unbothered. His phone was full of messages, some answered, some not. Invitations. Check-ins. A few goodbyes that didn't feel final but probably were. He ran a hand along his jaw and exhaled, the sound lost in the space.

He had money. A body people admired. A career that made his name ring in the right circles. Women who, on paper, were everything a man could ask for. He had mastered pursuit, momentum, achievement.

So why did his chest feel hollow?

He thought about Michelle 's eyes when she argued a point, about Elena's restless energy, Olivia's gaze lingering on canvas, Isabella's pencil scratching across paper, Aisha's voice when she talked about the universe. Pieces of something that still didn't feel whole, fragments that didn't assemble into a life.

The city lights blurred slightly as he stared, not from tears, just from fatigue he hadn't earned at the gym. For the first time, the view from the top felt less like a reward and more like a room with no door, all glass and no exit.

He turned away from the window, but the emptiness he was feeling deep inside, followed him into the darkness.

9

THE WOMEN WHO WALK AWAY

Jakil didn't plan for the night to end this way.

It started simple, just dinner... just catching up... just one more attempt at connection that he already knew would fall apart the same way the rest did.

Elena showed up first.

Not the Elena he'd called the wrong name weeks earlier.

Another Elena.

A nurse he'd met at a charity gala.

She looked tired tonight, her dark hair pulled into a loose bun, her makeup barely there. She didn't bother with a show. She didn't flirt. She didn't try to impress him.

She was just... herself.

And somehow, that made it worse.

They sat across from each other in a quiet corner of the restaurant, soft jazz humming in the background. Candles flickered between them, casting shadows across her face.

"Jakil," she said finally, pushing her half-finished wine aside, "you're trying to be present, but you're somewhere else."

He looked up. "I'm here."

"No," she whispered, shaking her head softly. "Your body is here. The rest of you is already gone."

The words hit harder than he expected.

He wanted to argue.

He wanted to deny it.

He wanted to be the man she deserved.

But he wasn't.

He'd never been.

She stood, lifted her purse, and placed a soft kiss on his cheek — a goodbye kiss, the kind that didn't hurt, but still managed to leave a mark.

"You're a good man, Jakil. But you're not ready."

And she walked away.

No fight.

No anger.

Just… truth.

He watched her leave until the door closed behind her.

Then came Michelle Patel — the lawyer, the firecracker, the woman who never let anyone waste her time. She called him outside the restaurant as he stepped into the night air. Her voice was sharp, brittle around the edges.

"I saw you on Instagram," she said. "Out last night with someone else. You don't even bother hiding it."

He closed his eyes, exhaling. "Michelle , it wasn't—"

"Don't lie."

Her tone cracked.

Just once.

"I thought maybe I misread things," she continued. "But you know what? I don't have the energy to compete with women who don't even know they're in the same race."

He didn't defend himself.

Didn't fight to keep her.

He didn't have the right.

"Goodbye, Jakil."

Another one gone.

Before he could even process it, his phone buzzed again.

Isabella.

Not angry.

Not crying.

Just done.

A single message:

"I need someone who chooses me. You choose noise. Be well."

He stared at the text until his screen dimmed.

Then… silence.

Real silence.

The kind that sinks into your bones.

The Silent Exit

When he got home, the penthouse felt unfamiliar—too wide, too quiet, too cold.

He tossed his keys on the marble counter and let out a slow breath. His footsteps echoed as he walked to the bedroom.

He didn't bother turning on the lights.

He sat on the edge of the bed, elbows on his knees, staring into the dark.

He had chased beauty.

He had chased thrill.

He had chased bodies, ambition, chemistry, validation.

But he hadn't chased love.

Not once.

And now every door behind him was closing.

One by one.

Quietly.

Firmly.

He wasn't being punished.

He wasn't being rejected.

He was being redirected.

Toward something… someone… softer.

Someone he hadn't met yet.

Someone who would change everything.

But tonight, he didn't feel destiny.

He felt loss.

A single tear slipped down his cheek, not from heartbreak, not from rejection... but from the dawning realization that he had built a life full of women and ended up completely alone.

The rain outside hit the windows in soft, rhythmic taps.

He listened to it, breathing slowly.

He didn't cry again.

Didn't break down.

Didn't collapse.

He just sat there.

Heavy.

Still.

And somewhere deep inside that silence, a small shift happened — something he almost didn't notice.

A readiness.

A want.

A quiet ache for something deeper.

Something real.

Something he didn't even believe he deserved yet.

He didn't know her name.

Didn't know her voice.

Didn't know her laugh or her smile or her story.

For the first time in years Jakil felt something unfamiliar rising inside him...

Hope.

10

THE SHIFT HE DIDN'T SEE COMING

The gym was nearly empty, the late-night crowd gone, replaced by dim lights and the echo of his own breathing. Jakil stood in front of the mirror, hands on his hips, sweat running down his temple. His reflection stared back at him. Broad shoulders. Clean lines. A body sculpted with intention; the kind people noticed without trying.

People always told him he looked strong.

Tonight, he didn't feel strong at all.

He wiped his face with a towel and exhaled slowly. The silence pressed in, thick and uncomfortable.

This wasn't burnout.

It wasn't depression.

It wasn't heartbreak.

It was something harder to name.

Emptiness.

For years, he had been that guy. The charismatic broker. The one with the penthouse, the tailored suits, the steady rotation of beautiful women. The man people watched when he walked into a room.

Now it all felt like a performance he'd forgotten how to step out of.

He sat on the bench, elbows on his knees, hands clasped together. A memory surfaced without warning. Elena in the elevator, eyes glassy, tears quiet and restrained. Not anger. Not drama. Just disappointment. The kind that lingered.

Then Aisha, smiling politely across a dinner table, already halfway gone. Choosing herself. Choosing her career. Not because she didn't care, but because she didn't trust him with something fragile.

Michelle turning away.

Isabella packing up her things.

Olivia leaving a gallery event early, pretending everything was fine.

Endings he hadn't argued against.

Moments he'd let slip without resistance.

He was the common thread.

"Damn," he muttered. "What am I doing?"

Not with his career. That part was solid.

Not with his body. He'd never been sharper.

But with everything else?

With what he gave people.

With what he kept for himself.

He didn't have an answer.

THE NEXT DAY, he met a client at a café in Georgetown. The kind of place with hanging plants, warm wood, and soft jazz humming just under the conversation. He arrived early and waited near the window.

A young couple sat a few tables away, sharing headphones, leaning into the same song. The girl rested her head on the guy's shoulder. He kissed the top of her hair without thinking.

It was small. Almost nothing.

It hit Jakil anyway.

Not desire.

Not jealousy.

Longing.

A quiet ache that caught him off guard. He looked away, rubbed the back of his neck, tried to shake it off.

He wasn't jealous of them.

He was jealous of how easy it looked.

No performance.

No strategy.

No walls.

Just comfort.

He realized then that he'd never had that. Not even close.

"I've never let anyone get that close," he admitted silently.

Over the next week, things he used to overlook started standing out.

A father holding his daughter's hand as they crossed the street.

An older couple splitting a pastry, smiling like they'd shared a lifetime of jokes.

A woman laughing on the phone, face lit up with something unguarded.

Everywhere he went, the same quiet theme surfaced.

Connection.

Not the kind he was good at creating. Not charm or attraction or chemistry that burned out fast.

Something slower.

Something rooted.

He found himself leaving parties early. Letting calls go unanswered. Deleting numbers he knew he wouldn't use. Declining dates he didn't have the energy to fake enthusiasm for.

His friends noticed.

"You good, Jak?"

"You been low-key lately."

"New situation or what?"

He just shrugged.

Nothing was wrong.

And yet, everything felt off.

. . .

ONE EVENING, on the walk home, a light rain started to fall. Not enough to run from. Just enough to notice. He didn't pull out an umbrella. He let it soak through his shirt, cool against his skin.

Halfway down the block, he stopped beneath a streetlamp.

Cars passed.

People hurried into cabs.

He stood there.

Breathing.

Listening.

Letting the quiet settle.

"I'm lonely," he admitted.

Not alone.

Lonely.

He had people. Attention. Options. He could fill his nights if he wanted to.

None of it touched him.

He didn't want more women.

He wanted one.

Someone who didn't feel like an audition.

Someone who saw past the image.

Someone who made him pause instead of perform.

Someone real.

He didn't know who that was. He didn't know if he was ready for it. He only knew the truth had finally caught up to him.

The rain kept falling.

Jakil started walking again.

Not toward anything specific.

Just forward.

Toward something he hadn't learned how to name yet.

11

EMPTY ROOMS

The first thing to go was the noise.

For years, Jakil's life had been full of it—ringing phones, buzzing messages, music, laughter, heels on hardwood floors, whispered promises in the dark. But now, nights fell quiet in his penthouse, and he found himself listening to the hum of the refrigerator like it was trying to tell him something.

He stopped counting how many days had passed since he'd last heard from Michelle . Or Olivia. Or Isabella. Or Elena. Or Aisha.

He just knew it had been long enough that the silence didn't feel temporary anymore. It felt permanent.

One night, after another long day of pretending everything was fine, he unlocked his door, dropped his keys on the entry table, and stood there without moving. The city lights spilled across his living room, stretching long shadows over expensive furniture that suddenly looked like props.

This place used to feel like proof he'd made it.

Now it just felt big.

Too big for one man with no one to share it with.

He walked to the kitchen, opened a cabinet, closed it again without taking anything out. He had food. He wasn't hungry. He had liquor. He didn't want to drink. Not tonight.

He ended up on the couch instead, elbows on his knees, hands clasped so tightly his knuckles went white.

For the first time, the thought pressed so hard against him he could barely breathe:

Maybe it was him.

Not the women.

Not timing.

Not "miscommunication."

Him.

He rose abruptly, grabbed his phone, and scrolled through his contacts. Michelle 's name. Elena's. Olivia's. Isabella's. Aisha's. More names after that—women he hadn't even thought about in weeks. Women he'd promised to call back. Women he'd taken out, charmed, tasted, and then quietly forgotten.

He stared at the screen for a long time.

Then, one by one, he started deleting.

Not just the five who mattered. All of them.

Each swipe felt like ripping off a bandage he'd been layering over a wound instead of treating. The more he deleted, the more naked his phone felt. The more naked he felt.

When he finished, he tossed the phone onto the couch and leaned back, staring up at the ceiling.

No backup plan.

No late-night "you up?" safety net.

Just him, And the echo of his empty room.

When sleep finally came, it was shallow and restless. He slept badly that night.

and woke up before dawn, heart racing, jaw tight. Sweat clung to his chest like he'd run a marathon in his dreams.

He dragged himself to the gym anyway.

The familiar clank of weights and the beat of music in his headphones usually centered him. Today, it didn't. He went through the motions—bench press, squats, rows—but his mind wasn't locked in. The mirror in front of him reflected a man who looked strong, composed, focused, but

he didn't feel any of those things.

Halfway through a set, he dropped the bar into the rack more clumsily than usual. A couple of guys glanced over, then looked away. He wiped his face with a towel and stared at his reflection.

"Who are you doing this for?" he muttered.

The answer used to be simple: for his body, his career, his image. For the version of himself people saw.

Now it felt hollow.

He cut the workout short and left.

Days blurred after that.

He went to work. He smiled for clients. He closed deals. He shook hands. He hosted open houses in condos that cost more than most people would make in ten years. He told couples, "You'll be happy here. This place is a fresh start."

The hypocrisy scraped at him.

At home, he tried to distract himself.

He turned on the TV and muted it. Flipped through channels he didn't watch. Sat with books open in his lap without turning the page. Opened dating apps he hadn't deleted yet… then closed them without logging in.

He thought, more than once, about calling one of the women he'd hurt. Just to apologize. Just to say, "You were right about me." Just to hear another human voice that wasn't about contracts or commissions.

He never dialed.

Instead, he did something he hadn't done in a while with his busy life, he called his mother.

She answered on the second ring, her voice warm and familiar. "My son. Look who remembers I exist."

He let out a breath that almost sounded like a laugh. "Ma."

"What's wrong?" she asked immediately.

"Why you assume something's wrong?"

"Because you only call me like this when you've done something stupid or something beautiful," she said. "And you don't sound happy."

He didn't talk about the women. Not directly. He didn't have the language for all of it yet. But he told her he'd been "messing up," that he'd hurt people, that he didn't like the man he was turning into.

She listened quietly, the way mothers do when they know pushing too hard will make you hang up.

Finally she said, "You are not a bad man, Jakil."

He swallowed. "I don't feel like a good one."

"Good men are not the ones who never hurt anybody," she replied. "They're the ones who look at the hurt and decide to change. Are you ready to change?"

He stared at his empty living room, at the windows, at the life he'd built.

"I think so," he said.

"Then start," she replied. "Not with them. With you."

After they hung up, the apartment didn't feel any less empty. But the emptiness felt… honest.

That night, he pulled a box out of his closet—old journals from college, books he kept saying he'd read when he had time. He sat on the floor with his back against the bed and opened one at random.

It wasn't a love story. It was a book about being alone. About who you are when nobody's watching. The kind of thing he used to roll his eyes at.

Now, he read every word.

A new routine formed, slowly and without announcement.

Work. Gym. Home. No women. No late-night hookups. No flirtatious strings left hanging for him to tug when he felt bored or lonely.

He started saying no.

No to drinks with colleagues who wanted to introduce him to, "someone perfect."

No to numbers scribbled on napkins.

No to invitations from women he knew would say yes, to whatever he suggested.

At first, it felt like punishment.

Then it felt like detox.

Weeks passed.

He noticed things he'd never paid attention to before: the way the city smelled different at dawn than at midnight; the old couple in his building who walked their dog holding hands; the way he always checked his reflection in glass doors before walking through them.

One evening, he was sitting on the arm of his couch, watching the sky darken, when a thought hit him so clearly it might as well have been spoken aloud.

He couldn't heal in the same life he'd hurt people in.

The penthouse.

The haunts.

The same restaurants.

The same routines.

He'd built this life on charm and rotation, on always having someone on standby. Now that it was gone, everything felt contaminated by who he'd been.

The idea came quietly at first.

A new city.

A new market.

A new start.

He pulled out his laptop and stared at the screen, the cursor blinking like it was daring him.

The brokerage he worked with had offices in a few major cities. One of them was Chicago.

He clicked the website and scrolled through the photos—skylines, neighborhoods, agents smiling in front of townhomes and high-rises. The city looked different from D.C. Rougher around the edges. Colder. Realer.

He searched rental listings, more out of curiosity than commitment. But as he clicked through, imagining himself in those spaces, something loosened in his chest.

He didn't book a flight that night.

Didn't submit a transfer request.

Didn't make any big decisions.

He just sat there, in the blue light of the laptop screen, thinking about starting over somewhere nobody knew him as the man who always had five women orbiting him.

Somewhere he could walk into a coffee shop and be just a guy ordering a drink, not a story someone warned their friends about.

For the first time in a long time, the idea of being unknown didn't scare him.

It felt… clean.

He closed the laptop, leaned his head back, and stared at the ceiling.

The rooms around him were still empty.

But the emptiness no longer felt like a verdict.

It felt like a blank page.

And for the first time, he wondered what might happen if, somewhere out there, a woman saw him not as the man he had been…

…but as the man he was finally trying to become.

WITHIN DAYS, the decision made itself.

Chicago wasn't an escape. It was a reset—with structure. Six months. A temporary office assignment. Long enough to step away without dismantling the life he'd built.

He moved the way he always did—clean, decisive, quiet.

He found another penthouse overlooking the city, comparable to the one he owned. Floor-to-ceiling windows. Controlled silence. Space that felt private instead of performative. A high-end car followed soon after, low profile tires, polished to a high gloss to reflect the sun rays, unmistakably his. Nothing about the move was small.

What changed was the intention.

He wanted a place where he could work, lift, come home, and exist without interruption. No expectations. No explanations. Just room to think.

On his second morning in the city, he searched for a gym.

Not a chain. Not a scene. Something independent.

He found a startup space in the south loop—new equipment, unfinished details, the kind of place still finding its footing. Midday, it was quiet. A few lifters. No front desk. Just a man adjusting plates near the racks.

"You the owner?" Jakil asked.

The man nodded. "Yeah. Just opened."

Jakil worked out without drawing attention. The space wasn't flashy, but it was solid. When he finished, the owner approached him.

"I Appreciate you stopping by," the man said. "I'm Marcus."

"Jakil."

They shook hands and exchanged a few words. Nothing personal. Just business, logistics, the reality of starting something from scratch.

Jakil came back the next day. And the next.

By the end of the week, he stayed after his workout.

"You ever consider a silent partner?" he asked the owner.

Marcus studied him. "Depends on the terms."

They sat down in the office—bare walls, temporary furniture, ambition filling the gaps.

Jakil was direct. He told him he was in the city for six months. That he had capital he needed to place before tax season. That he wasn't interested in managing, branding, or being visible.

"I just want access," Jakil said. "My own keys. I come and go as I please."

Marcus nodded slowly. "That's workable."

They finalized the agreement days later.

The key felt heavier than it should have when Jakil added it to his ring.

Not because it meant ownership—but because it meant privacy.

A place to train.

A place to clear his head.

A place that didn't know his history.

At night, back in his penthouse, the city stretched out below him—different skyline, same quiet. He poured himself a drink and stood at the floor to ceilings windows, letting the stillness settle.

Chicago didn't feel like a mistake.

It felt intentional.

And for the first time in a long time, the life he was living, felt like one he'd chosen, not one he had fallen into.

12

THE COFFEE SHOP MOMENT

Kayla dragged herself out of bed that Saturday morning, the kind of morning where the air felt heavy before she even opened the blinds. She shuffled into her softest hoodie, tied her hair into a loose bun, and left the apartment without even checking the mirror. She didn't care. She just fresh needed air, and caffeine. Preferably in that order.

The neighborhood coffee shop was warm and buzzing with weekend energy, typing on laptops, quiet conversations, and soft jazz coming from the overhead speakers. The kinds of sounds that made the world feel slightly safer than it really was.

Kayla moved to the back of the line and tugged her sleeves over her hands. She wasn't looking for anything or anyone. She barely had the energy to look at the menu. Her mind still sat in the dark corner where she'd left it the night before, replaying the same questions she wished she could turn off.

Then the door opened, and something shifted.

A man walked in—tall, broad-shouldered, moving with a quiet confidence that didn't ask for attention but pulled it anyway. He had smooth brown skin, a neatly trimmed beard, and an energy that settled over the room like gravity.

For a moment, the coffee shop seemed to lean toward him.

Kayla didn't recognize him, but something inside her jolted as if she should have. Like her spirit stood up straighter even though her body didn't move at all.

He stepped into line behind her, close enough that she could feel his presence, but far enough to show he wasn't intruding. His voice, when he ordered, was low and calm, almost soothing. She didn't turn around. She couldn't. She suddenly became painfully aware of her hoodie, her bare face, her messy bun. If he looked at her right now, she might collapse into the floor.

The barista said his name when she handed him his drink.

Jakil, a simple name. A strong one. It fit him.

Kayla inhaled slowly, hoping he didn't hear the tremble in her breath. When she picked up her own drink and turned to leave, she angled her body so she wouldn't have to face him directly. She wanted to disappear before he could see her. Before he could confirm what she already feared—that she wasn't the kind of woman men noticed.

She caught only a glimpse of him in her peripheral vision.

He wasn't looking her way;

Never glanced in her direction.

He didn't even know she existed.

And somehow, that made her chest ache more than she expected.

Kayla slipped out the door, the cold air meeting her warm cheeks. She walked down the sidewalk, her drink clutched against her chest, breathing deeply as she tried to shake the feeling that she'd just brushed against something bigger than her.

She didn't know why he affected her. He hadn't said a word to her. He hadn't even looked at her. But something about him lingered—like a memory that hadn't happened yet, like a chord that was plucked inside her without permission.

She kept walking, but her steps felt unsteady, her heartbeat too loud in her ears. Something was stirring inside her, something she wasn't ready to name. She didn't know if this moment meant anything. She didn't even understand why it mattered.

But it did.

She felt it.

Kayla reached the corner and paused, looking down at the sidewalk as a slow breath left her lungs. The city moved around her—cars, footsteps, voices—but she felt strangely still.

For the first time in a long time, something shifted in her. Not hope, not love, not fantasy. Just a flicker. Like someone had cracked open a window she didn't realize was sealed shut.

She lifted her drink and took a slow sip, the warmth coating her throat.

The wind brushed her cheek.

And for the briefest moment, she wondered who he was…

and why her heart reacted like it already knew him.

She kept walking, but the thought stayed with her, soft and persistent, refusing to let go.

13

FRAGMENTS OF THE WOMEN HE LOST

Before Kayla

Before Chicago.

Before the quiet turning point in that coffee shop…

There were the women who walked in and out of Jakil's life, but not before leaving fingerprints on him.

Some bruised.

Some tender.

Some unforgettable.

Some he wished he could forget.

It happened on a rainy Tuesday, during a fine, misty rain that made the whole city look blurred.

Michelle showed up at his place without warning.

He opened the door smiling, ready with a joke, but one look at her face wiped the humor clean off him.

She wasn't angry.

She wasn't dramatic.

She was… tired.

"Jakil," she said softly, "I can't keep trying to guess if you care about me or if I'm just one of the women you rotate."

He reached for her. "Michelle , it's not like—"

She stepped back.

That small movement—barely a shuffle—felt louder than a slap.

She wasn't wearing makeup. Her hair was messy from the rain. She looked real. More real than he'd ever seen her.

"You're a good man, Jakil," she whispered. "But you're not a ready man."

And she walked away.

No shouting.

No last kiss.

No dramatic exit.

Just a quiet, final closing of a door he never opened again.

ELENA WAS fire from the beginning.

So it made sense that their ending burned, too.

She found the messages—flirty texts from another woman he'd forgotten to delete.

Nothing explicitly scandalous.

But enough.

She confronted him in his living room, pacing back and forth, hands trembling, voice cracking between anger and heartbreak.

"You tested me. You opened up to me. You made me think I was someone special."

Her laugh was sharp, bitter.

"And all that time you were collecting women like business cards."

"Elena—please—"

"No," she snapped, picking up her purse. "If you want to be a player, then own it. But don't pretend you're looking for a soulmate."

She didn't slam the door when she left.

She closed it like she was sealing a tomb.

. . .

OLIVIA's Silent Exit

Olivia didn't yell.

Didn't cry.

Didn't argue.

She simply stopped answering his messages.

One night, he saw her across a crowded gallery, standing beside another man—someone soft-faced and artistic, the kind of guy who probably remembered anniversaries and brought her flowers just because.

She spotted Jakil.

Their eyes met.

She gave him the smallest nod—one that said:

I'm choosing better for myself.

And then she walked away.

The silence she left behind was the loudest breakup he'd ever had.

ISABELL A, The One Who Wanted More

Their ending happened at the most unexpected moment—during a beautiful road trip he planned thinking it would deepen their connection.

They were parked by a scenic overlook, city lights glittering far below them.

Isabella leaned on the railing, hair blowing in the wind, eyes soft but sad.

"You don't love me," she said quietly.

He blinked. "I never said I did."

"That's the problem," she murmured. "I do, Jakil. Or I'm falling. And you… you're standing still."

He didn't know what to say.

Isabella wiped a tear he hadn't noticed.

She kissed his cheek—slow, lingering, almost grateful—and whispered:

"You are meant to love someone deeply. But it isn't me."

She drove them back in silence.

The next morning, she returned his key.

ASIAH, was the most mature of them all. Maybe that's why her ending hurt so differently. It was colder and cleaner.

They sat across from each other at a café. She stirred her tea slowly, eyes focused on the swirling liquid instead of him.

"I got the research grant," she said softly. "I'm leaving for Geneva."

"That's incredible," he said honestly. "But… us?"

She met his eyes finally.

"There is no 'us,' Jakil. Not really. I know it. You know it."

He swallowed. "Maybe I can—"

"No," she cut in, gently but firmly. "You need to grow. And I need to go."

She reached across the table, placing her warm hand over his.

"I care about you. Enough to walk away before I resent you."

He didn't try to stop her.

For once, he knew letting go was the kindest thing he could do.

Wounds He Didn't Notice Until Later

A night where a woman left crying because another woman's earring was found under his bed.

A brunch date where he flirted with the waitress out of habit—then realized the pain in the woman sitting across from him.

A birthday he forgot.

A promise he broke.

A plan he canceled last second.

A lipstick stain that wasn't his date's color.

A dozen moments where he should have been a man…

and instead acted like a boy with muscles and money.

ONE QUIET NIGHT While sitting alone at his kitchen counter, lights off, drinking water from a glass like it's the first drink he's had in years,

Jakil had only one thought echoing in his head:

All of those endings had one common denominator—"me".

The weight of that truth finally settled in his chest, heavy and honest.

For the first time…

He understood the difference between loneliness and being alone.

He wasn't lonely.

He was emptied out.

Now he was ready, finally, for something real and something rare.

14

A MAN IN TRANSITION

The morning after all the exits felt different.

Not sharp.

Not painful.

Just… hollow.

Jakil woke before sunrise, not because he was rested, but because sleep no longer wanted him. His body rose slowly from the bed, heavy and unmotivated, as if gravity had increased overnight. The city outside his penthouse windows hovered in a quiet in-between state, neither night nor morning, washed in a pale orange haze that felt hesitant, like even the light wasn't sure it belonged yet.

He sat on the edge of the mattress, elbows resting on his thighs, rubbing his face with both hands. His skin felt tight. Dry. Older than it should have. The silence pressed in around him, thick and unmoving.

For the first time in a long time, the quiet didn't feel earned.

It felt like consequence.

He walked barefoot through the apartment, the cool floor grounding him with each step. The space was immaculate, curated, designed to impress people who rarely stayed long enough to care. Furniture placed just right. Art chosen for impact. Everything polished. Everything distant.

He stopped at the floor-to-ceiling windows.

Chicago, Illinois looked softened at this hour. Streets barely moving. Cars whispering instead of roaring. Steam rising lazily from vents like the city itself exhaling. The sky shifted slowly from deep blue to muted gold, stretching into the day without urgency.

Jakil pressed his palm against the glass.

"Who the hell am I becoming?" he whispered.

The words didn't echo. The room absorbed them.

His reflection hovered faintly in the glass. Handsome. Disciplined. Controlled. The man people admired without asking questions. He saw the sharp jaw, the wide shoulders, the sculpted body women chased and men respected.

And behind it all, he saw the exhaustion.

The loneliness no one ever looked for.

He left the apartment earlier than usual, driving to the gym before the city had fully woken up. The parking lot was nearly empty, his car sitting alone beneath flickering streetlights. Inside, the gym lights hummed harshly, fluorescent and unforgiving. The air smelled like metal, rubber mats, and effort.

He wrapped his wrists out of habit, movements automatic, practiced. Grabbed dumbbells. Started his routine.

Bench.

Rows.

Shoulders.

His body obeyed.

His mind didn't.

The weights felt heavier than they should have. Not physically — emotionally. The burn didn't focus him. The sweat didn't cleanse him. Each rep felt like repetition instead of purpose.

Halfway through a set, he stopped.

Dropped the weights back into the rack harder than necessary.

He leaned forward, hands braced on his knees, breath coming faster than the effort required. His reflection stared back at him in the mirror — strong, controlled, put together.

And completely disconnected.

For the first time, the gym didn't feel like discipline.

It felt like avoidance.

He wasn't running toward something.

He was running from himself, and he could feel it gaining ground.

His phone buzzed on the bench.

Once.

He ignored it.

Again.

Again.

Annoyance flared until he grabbed it — and froze.

Aisha Khan.

The name landed with unexpected weight.

Brilliant.

Independent.

Unapologetically certain.

The one who had chosen her future without hesitation.

The one who had walked away clean.

He hadn't expected to hear from her again.

Ever.

He answered slowly.

"Hey."

Her voice was calm. Familiar. Unchanged.

"Hi, Jakil."

Silence followed — deliberate, uncomfortable, forcing space open between them.

"I don't want anything from you," she said. "I just wanted to say… you're not a bad man. But you're a man who doesn't know what he wants."

He closed his eyes.

She continued, each word measured, precise.

"And until you figure that out, you're going to keep hurting people. Not intentionally. But consistently."

He said nothing.

There was nothing left to defend.

"I hope you find someone who makes you slow down enough to

feel," Aisha said. "Someone who isn't impressed by your body or your success. Someone who makes you choose her — only her."

Her voice softened, just slightly.

"Because that's the only way you'll ever be truly happy."

His throat tightened.

"Thank you," he whispered.

It was the most honest thing he'd said in months.

The line clicked off.

He stared at the phone long after the screen dimmed, her words settling into him slowly, deliberately — not accusing, just true.

After leaving the gym, Jakil didn't drive home.

He didn't know where he was going until he was already walking.

City blocks blended together. Coffee shops lifting their gates. Street vendors setting up. Morning joggers threading past him with purpose he didn't have.

His thoughts raced.

His steps slowed.

Memories surfaced in fragments — laughter, dinners, bedsheets, arguments, confusion. Different women. Same ending.

He wanted something real.

But he didn't know how to be real.

Not yet.

He stopped near a busy corner, leaning against a railing. A bus hissed beside him, doors opening, releasing people into the morning — a mother guiding a stroller, a man lost in music, a teenage girl buried in her hoodie.

And then —

Laughter.

Soft.

Warm.

Unforced.

It pulled at him before he could stop it.

He turned to see who it was.

Across the street, a group of women spilled out of a breakfast spot, voices overlapping, bodies moving with easy familiarity. He couldn't see their faces clearly. Just energy. Motion.

But one stood out.

Something about her presence made him straighten. Made his breath shift. She threw her head back in laughter — deep, unfiltered, real.

Even through traffic, he felt it, a pull.

HE STEPPED FORWARD INSTINCTIVELY — but a delivery truck rolled past, blocking his view for a heartbeat.

When it cleared —

She was gone.

Turning the corner with her friends, disappearing into the morning.

He stood there longer than necessary; eyes fixed on empty space.

She left behind a feeling.

A whisper.

A question he couldn't answer.

Who was she?

The city surged around him.

But Jakil didn't move.

Something electric spread beneath his ribs.

He'd never seen her face.

Didn't know her voice.

Didn't know her name.

Yet somehow…

HE KNEW one day their paths would cross, and somehow, she would matter.

15

WHEN PATHS START MOVING

Jakil couldn't shake it.

That moment on the sidewalk — that flash of a woman laughing with her friends — it clung to him like perfume on a collar.

Not overwhelming.

Just… there.

Soft but persistent.

It followed him into the elevator. Into his office. Into the quiet pauses between phone calls where his mind usually snapped back into control. By the afternoon, he found himself standing at the window of his office, staring down at the city instead of answering emails that normally commanded his full attention. Traffic crawled below, people moving with purpose, unaware of how easily a life could tilt off balance in a single second.

His assistant, Monica, poked her head in once, then again, concern etched lightly across her face.

"You okay?" she asked, careful not to push.

He nodded both times. Reflexive. Automatic.

But the truth sat heavier.

He wasn't sure.

Because for the first time in a long time, he felt something that didn't arrive wrapped in logic or desire or control. It wasn't lust. It wasn't curiosity. It didn't ask for anything.

It simply *existed.*

And Jakil hated things that didn't make sense.

THAT EVENING, he did what he always did when something unsettled him.

He pushed his body harder.

A second workout. Heavier weights. Faster pace. Shorter rest between sets. The gym lights glared down as sweat ran into his eyes, his muscles trembling under the strain. The treadmill numbers climbed. His lungs burned. His heartbeat thundered in his ears.

Normally, this would clear his head. Strip everything down to breath and effort.

Tonight, it didn't.

Every time he closed his eyes, the image floated back in.

That woman.

That laugh.

That energy.

Man, get a grip, he told himself.

He didn't know her name.

Didn't know her voice.

Didn't know anything real.

And yet, the feeling refused to leave.

Across the City Kayla sat at her dining table, laptop open, half-finished tea cooling beside her. She edited product descriptions for her skincare line, rereading the same sentence three times before realizing she wasn't absorbing it.

Earlier, Jasmine had texted her:

"Girl, your stuff smells good enough to make a man propose. Keep pushing."

Lisa sent a long voice note about a client meltdown that spiraled into unrelated gossip.

Sarah dropped stock advice she barely understood but appreciated anyway.

Michelle flooded the group chat with memes.

Her girls were loud, chaotic, brilliant — and without even trying, they anchored her.

She smiled. Responded. Laughed quietly to herself.

But when the messages slowed…

When the house settled…

When the familiar hum of night took over…

Something crept in.

Not the usual loneliness.

Not insecurity.

Not the ache she'd learned how to carry.

This felt different.

Like something had brushed past her spirit without touching her skin. Like a door had opened somewhere she hadn't known existed.

She didn't question it.

Didn't analyze it.

She wrapped a blanket around her shoulders, opened the window, and let the cool night breeze press against her face, grounding her.

Back in his penthouse, Jakil sat on the edge of his bed long after midnight. The city glowed beneath him, distant and untouchable. His room stayed dark, lit only by reflections of traffic lights against the glass.

He ran a hand along his jaw, slower than usual.

He never obsessed over strangers.

Never replayed moments.

Never lingered on things that hadn't already offered him something tangible.

But this felt like he'd missed something.

Something important.

Something meant for him.

It stirred something he'd buried beneath years of temporary

women and temporary feelings — a part of himself that remembered wanting connection without conquest.

He exhaled slowly.

"Who are you?" he whispered into the dark.

The words sounded foolish.

And yet… he meant them.

THE NEXT MORNING, Jakil woke early, restless energy buzzing beneath his skin. He grabbed coffee from his usual spot, barely tasting it. Even the barista noticed.

"You good?" she asked, eyebrow raised.

He forced a smile. "Just thinking."

On the way to the office, he caught sight of a woman on a bus with the same hairstyle. His chest jumped. Palms dampened. His body reacted before his mind could catch up.

As the bus rolled closer…

It wasn't her.

Disappointment settled heavier than it had any right to.

This was ridiculous.

He didn't know her.

Had never spoken to her.

Had only seen her for seconds across a street.

But sometimes destiny didn't announce itself with fireworks. Sometimes it whispered, barely audible, just enough to make you turn your head.

KAYLA ARRIVED AT WORK LATE — which bothered her more than she admitted. She blamed traffic. The coffee line. Anything except the truth.

She hadn't slept well.

Her thoughts had wandered. Her spirit felt like it had taken a step ahead of her body, tugging her forward without explanation.

In the office elevator, she caught her reflection in the mirrored wall.

"Get it together, Kay," she murmured with a small smile.

But the woman looking back had a softness in her eyes she didn't recognize yet, not weakness, not longing, but awareness.

AROUND NOON, Jakil stepped out for lunch, his strides longer than usual. He didn't know why he turned down that street. He didn't have a destination in mind.

At the same time, Kayla left her office with coworkers, heading toward a café nearby — the same one Jakil happened to be walking toward.

Neither of them saw the other.

Not yet.

But the distance between them shortened.

The rhythm aligned.

The world nudged them closer without permission.

The universe didn't always shout.

Sometimes it whispered.

Sometimes it nudged.

Sometimes it let two people pass within fifty feet of each other without meeting,

just so the eventual collision… would feel inevitable.

16

CLOSE ENOUGH TO TOUCH

The weather shifted that Friday morning, not dramatically, just enough to make the air feel charged, like the city was holding its breath. Jack woke up unusually early, long before his alarm. He lay staring at the ceiling, a restless energy pulsing through him.

He didn't know why, but something in his chest felt unsettled. He showered longer than usual, picked a shirt, then changed it, put on cologne, then added another spray, like he was trying too hard, and hated himself for it.

Man, what is wrong with you? he muttered, shaking his head.

He didn't have an answer, but some part of him felt like today mattered.

On the other side of the city, Kayla pressed her forehead to the bathroom mirror at work, because she felt off, not sad, not anxious_ Just on edge, like her spirit was pacing. She brushed her curls back, reapplied lip gloss, and whispered to her reflection, *You're okay. You're good.* But she didn't sound convinced.

When she walked back to her desk, Jasmine texted her.

You coming to the café with us later?

Yeah, Kayla replied.

I need fresh air.

You need a man.

Kayla rolled her eyes and smiled, but her heart whispered a softer truth. *I need something.* She just didn't know what yet.

Kayla left the office late. The sky was already dim, streetlights flickering on one by one like small blessings. Her heels clicked against the sidewalk in a tired rhythm, the kind that said she'd given the world more than she had to spare today. Her girls had invited her out after work, but she turned them down. She needed silence. She needed clarity. She needed something she couldn't name.

Her phone buzzed.

You sure you don't want to come? We're doing tacos and tequila.

Kayla smiled gently and texted back. *Another night. I'm okay.*

She wasn't lying, but she wasn't telling the whole truth either. She was tired of being the funny one, the caring one, the invisible one. She wanted more, but she didn't know where to find it.

As she rounded the corner toward her car, she wasn't watching where she was going. She was digging for her keys, juggling her bag, muttering at herself, which is exactly why she bumped into someone hard.

Her bag slipped; papers scattered. Kayla gasped.

"Oh, I'm so sorry, I didn't—"

Her voice froze.

The man she'd collided with had stepped forward, steadying her. He was tall. Clean-cut. Deep brown skin, broad shoulders. A quiet but powerful presence that made the air tighten around him.

"No, no, it was my fault, are you all right?" he said. His voice was smooth, low, effortless. Calm.

Kayla blinked twice, her heart drumming like it wanted out of her chest.

"Yes. I'm fine."

He crouched down to help gather her papers. She crouched too. Their hands brushed once. It was nothing, but it was everything. She pulled her hand back quickly, like the touch was too much and not enough at the same time.

He noticed her flustered breath. She noticed the warmth in his eyes.

Something unfamiliar and electric, passed between them. Not a spark, but a recognition, like meeting someone your soul already knew.

He held out the last paper. "Here you go."

Kayla swallowed; her voice barely steady. "Thank you."

They both stood. He extended his hand.

"I'm Jakil."

She placed her hand in his, nervous but pretending not to be.

"And I'm Kayla"

... Kayla.

The way he said her name, soft, curious, slow, made her knees weaken.

"Pretty name."

She looked down, hiding a blush. She hoped he didn't see it. He did, and he liked it more than he expected.

Silence stretched between them. Not awkward, not heavy. Just full.

Finally, Jack slid his hands into his pockets, studying her in a way that made her feel seen, really seen.

"You heading home?"

"Yeah," she said. "Long day."

He nodded. "I get that."

Another small beat. Another tightening of something they couldn't explain.

Kayla forced a smile. "Well, thank you again." She began to turn away, but he stopped her softly.

"Kayla."

She turned back. Her heartbeat stuttered.

"Can I ask you something?"

"Sure."

"You ever go to that café on Monroe? The one with the ugly yellow awning?"

She laughed. It slipped out before she could stop it. "All the time."

"Thought so. I think I've seen you there."

Her breath caught. She didn't remember seeing him, but she felt something every time she went. Now it made sense.

He gave her a small, crooked smile. "Maybe I'll see you there again."

She swallowed. "Maybe."

He didn't move until she opened her car door. She didn't move until she knew he couldn't see her trembling hands.

They were strangers. Complete strangers. And yet, tonight the world felt suddenly different. Bigger. Brighter. Possibly dangerous.

Kayla drove away with her heart in her throat, whispering to herself, *Don't get excited. Don't get excited.*

She already was.

Jakil watched her taillights fade, wondering why it felt like something important had just walked into his life, and why he wasn't sure he was ready for it.

Kayla didn't sleep much after running into Jakil. Her mind spun all night, replaying the moment they met. The way his voice wrapped around her name. The warmth of his hand when it brushed hers.

She told herself not to get excited, but she failed. Her stomach fluttered every time she thought about him. The next morning, she dressed slower than usual, checking her mirror twice, then again. Not because she expected to see him, but because she hoped.

The day dragged until lunchtime.

Jasmine nudged her at her desk. "You're acting weird today."

"I don't act weird," Kayla smirked.

"You don't act weird unless a man is involved."

"I don't even know him like that."

"But you want to."

Kayla didn't answer. She didn't have to.

When she walked to the café that afternoon, she tried to convince herself she wasn't looking around. It didn't matter. Her eyes scanned every inch of the place anyway.

And there he was.

Jack sat alone at a small table near the window, scrolling his phone, an empty iced coffee beside him. Clean haircut. Black fitted tee. Forearms that made her forget how to breathe.

He lifted his eyes, saw her, and the soft smile he gave made Kayla's chest tighten.

He stood. "Kayla."

"Hi," she said, trying not to sound breathless. "Didn't expect to see you."

"I was hoping I would."

That threw her off balance just a little.

They sat across from each other. The conversation flowed easily. Work. The city. Favorite foods. Dream vacations.

He listened when she spoke. Really listened. No man had ever made her feel that before.

Then his expression shifted. Not harsh. Not judgmental. Just serious.

"Can I ask you something personal?"

Kayla swallowed. "Depends how personal."

He leaned forward slightly. "You ever think about changing your lifestyle? Like fitness?"

She froze. It was the topic she avoided, the insecurity she carried like a secret wound.

"I mean," she said carefully, "I try sometimes. It never sticks."

He held her gaze. "You know I'm a trainer too, right? I see potential in people. And when I look at you, I see more than what you see."

Her chest tightened. "I don't want to be someone's project."

"You're not," he said softly. "But if you ever wanted help, I'd give it to you."

She looked down at her cup, fidgeting with the lid. "Why me?"

"Because you're beautiful," he said without hesitation. "And because I see someone powerful under everything you don't like about yourself. I want to show you what I see."

Her heart pounded so hard she felt it in her neck.

"I don't know," she whispered. "Training is a lot."

"So don't think about the whole mountain," he said. "Think about the first step. Let me train you. Give me a few weeks. See how you feel."

"What if I can't do it?"

"That's impossible," he said. "I've trained hundreds of people, and none of them had your heart."

The compliment hit her deeper than she expected. She wiped her palms on her jeans, her breath shaky.

"You really think I could change?"

"I know you can."

Silence hovered between them. Tender. Warm. Scary.

Finally, she whispered, "Okay."

His eyes lit up.

"Yeah?"

She nodded. "Yeah. I'll try."

He smiled slow, proud, like he already saw the future version of her she couldn't see yet.

"You won't regret it."

Kayla wasn't so sure, but for the first time in a long time, she felt hope. Real hope.

And that was enough to change everything.

17

DAY ONE HURTS

Kayla regretted saying yes, the moment she walked into Jakil's gym.

It wasn't the equipment that intimidated her. It was the people — all the sculpted bodies, tight leggings, defined arms, perfect confidence dripping off every machine. Kayla felt like she had walked into a world that didn't belong to her.

But then she saw him.

Jakil stood near the back, wiping down a bench, his shoulders broad and secure. When he noticed her, his face softened instantly.

"Kayla," he said, walking toward her. "You showed up."

"I almost didn't," she admitted.

He laughed gently. "Most people don't. That's why I respect the ones who do."

His reassurance calmed her for all of six seconds… until he clapped his hands together.

"Alright. Let's get started."

That's when the suffering began.

First was the treadmill.

She lasted five minutes before her chest burned like she'd swallowed fire. She slowed to a walk, wheezing.

"I can't breathe," she gasped.

"You're breathing," he said calmly. "Keep walking."

"I'm dying."

"You're talking, so you're not dying."

She shot him a look. He grinned. It almost helped — almost.

Next came squats.

Her thighs screamed. Her knees begged for mercy. She felt sweat dripping into places she didn't know could sweat.

"Why do people do this willingly?" she demanded.

"Because they want the results," he said.

"I want the results too, but I don't want to die for them."

He smiled. "You're not dying."

"Feels like it."

Then came the weights. Small ones. Light ones. But by the tenth rep, Kayla's arms shook like they were made of jelly.

"I can't lift this," she panted.

"Yes you can," he said.

"No I can't."

"Yes you can. One more."

She scowled. "I hate you."

He chuckled. "Later you'll thank me."

"Later I'm going to block your number."

He laughed so loudly the woman next to them turned and smiled.

Kayla tried to laugh too… but mostly she just tried not to throw up.

By the time the session ended, she couldn't lift her water bottle. She leaned against the wall, face flushed, chest rising and falling in unsteady rhythm.

"This," she said breathlessly, "was a mistake."

Jakil crouched so his eyes were level with hers.

"Kayla," he said softly. "I'm proud of you."

Her eyes widened. "Why? I barely did anything."

"You showed up," he said. "And you didn't quit."

She swallowed hard. Something about his tone — gentle, sincere — hit deeper than she expected.

"I feel like I'm gonna pass out," she said.

"You won't."

"I might."

"If you pass out, I'll catch you."

She forced a smile. "You say that to all your clients?"

"No," he said quietly. "Just you."

Her heart skipped.

She looked down, unable to hold the intensity of his gaze. "I'm not used to this," she whispered.

"Used to what?"

"Someone believing I can do something hard."

He didn't hesitate. "Get used to it. Because I'm not going anywhere."

Emotion rose in her chest so quickly she wasn't ready for it.

She blinked fast, trying to swallow it back. But one tear escaped anyway.

He noticed.

And he did something unexpected.

He didn't comfort her.

He didn't make it emotional.

He simply said:

"This is day one. It's supposed to hurt. But every day you show up, it'll hurt a little less. And then one day… you'll shock yourself."

Kayla wiped the tear quickly. "Why are you being so nice to me?"

He looked at her for a long moment, like he wasn't sure if he should say what he was thinking.

But then he did.

"Because I see who you're going to become," he said. "And I want you to see her too."

Her breath caught.

She didn't know how to respond… so she didn't.

She just nodded.

She would show up tomorrow.

And the next day.

And the next.

She didn't know it yet…
but this was the beginning of everything.

KAYLA WOKE up the next morning and instantly regretted it.

Every muscle in her body screamed. Her thighs felt like someone had set them on fire. Her arms wouldn't lift above her shoulders. Even her eyelashes felt heavy.

She groaned as she rolled out of bed.

"This is what hell feels like," she muttered.

But she got dressed anyway.

Pulled her hair up.

Swallowed her pride, and drove to the gym.

She wasn't ready for day two…

but something in her refused to quit.

When she walked in, Jakil was already there, leaning against the counter, sipping a protein shake. He looked up and his whole face lit.

"You came back."

"Barely," she said. "I almost called 911 on myself."

He laughed. "That means yesterday worked."

"No, that means I should sue you."

He shook his head. "Stretch first. Then we'll warm up."

She stretched.

She whimpered.

He smirked.

Then came the treadmill.

"Two minutes jogging, one minute walking," he said.

Kayla stared at him like he'd lost his entire mind. "Jogging? I don't jog. I briskly walk. Sometimes."

"You're jogging today."

"No I'm not."

"Yes you are."

She jogged.

Badly.

Her feet slapped the treadmill like she was trying to stomp out demons. Her breathing turned into a wheeze.

"Oh God!" she yelped. "This thing is trying to kill me."

Jakil laughed so hard he had to cover his mouth.

"You alright?" he asked.

"No!" she snapped. "And stop laughing at me!"

He wiped a tear from his eye. "I'm not laughing at you. I'm laughing with—"

"I am not laughing!"

That made him laugh harder.

She glared at him…

but deep down, she loved that he wasn't treating her like she was fragile.

When the treadmill torture was over, they moved on to weights. And that's when everything changed.

Halfway through a shoulder press, Kayla dropped the dumbbells with a loud clatter and stepped away, hands on her hips, chest tight.

"Kayla?" he asked, tone shifting instantly.

She shook her head. "I can't do this."

"Yes you can."

"No, I really can't." Her voice cracked. "My body isn't built for this."

"It is."

"No it's not!" Her face twisted. "I feel stupid. Everyone else in here looks perfect and I look like—"

"Don't do that," he said sharply.

She swallowed. Hard.

But the tears came anyway.

Hot. Uninvited. Fast.

"I'm tired," she whispered. "I'm tired of being the biggest one everywhere I go. I'm tired of pretending I'm okay with it. I'm tired of trying to love myself when half the time I don't even like myself."

Jakil stepped closer.

Not too close.

Just enough.

"Look at me," he said.

She hesitated. Then finally raised her eyes.

His voice softened. "You're not weak. You're not slow. You're not behind. You're not less than anyone in this building."

She blinked, tears rolling silently.

"You're just at day two," he said. "And the only difference between you and them… is that you're brave enough to start."

Her lip trembled. She turned her face away, but he gently guided it back with two fingers under her chin.

"Hey," he whispered. "Don't hide from me."

Her breath shook. "Why do you care so much?"

He opened his mouth… then closed it.

He didn't even know how to explain it yet.

So he said the only truth he had.

"Because you matter," he whispered. "More than you realize."

Kayla's tears fell faster then — not because she was broken…

but because she was starting to believe him.

Just a little.

He wiped one of her tears with his thumb. "Give me one more rep."

She sniffed. "Just one?"

"Just one."

"Fine."

She lifted the weight. Slowly. Painfully. But she did it.

"There you go," he said proudly.

Kayla exhaled, her heartbeat slowing. "Okay… maybe I don't hate this."

"You don't hate me either," he teased.

She rolled her eyes. "I might."

He laughed, grabbing a towel for her. "Day two is done."

She took the towel and met his eyes.

"No," she said softly. "Day two I managed to survive."

He smiled at her, like she'd just told him something important,

And maybe, she had…

18

THE HUNGER, THE HEAT, AND THE HARD TRUTHS

By the end of the first week, Kayla was exhausted in ways she didn't even know existed.

Her legs hurt.

Her arms hurt.

Her back hurt.

Her feelings hurt.

But nothing—absolutely nothing—hurt more than the hunger.

It wasn't the neat little hunger you could tame with a glass of water. It was the kind that didn't stay in her stomach, the kind that climbed up into her head and sat behind her eyes. It showed up at night when the apartment was quiet, when the world wasn't asking her to be strong, when she didn't have to smile or nod or pretend, she was fine.

Real hunger.

The kind that felt like a voice. A sweet, familiar one. The same voice that had comforted her after bad days, awkward days, lonely days, days where she'd tried to be "good" and still felt invisible.

Come on, girl... just a little snack... nobody will know...

She tried. She really did.

She packed her meals like Jakil told her. She lined them up in plastic containers like a promise she wasn't sure she could keep. She meal-prepped grilled chicken and broccoli until the smell of it started to feel personal, like the food itself was judging her. She measured portions. She read labels. She tracked everything like it was a job.

She drank water until she felt like she was floating.

And still, the hunger stayed.

It didn't feel like her body needed fuel. It felt like her heart needed comfort, and her brain didn't know how to ask for it without reaching for sugar, salt, bread, softness, anything that quieted her thoughts for five minutes.

By Thursday night, her discipline was frayed around the edges.

She walked into her kitchen, turned on the overhead light, and immediately wished she hadn't. Bright lights made every flaw feel louder. The counters were clean, the sink empty, the apartment still. She opened the refrigerator and stared.

There it was.

A slice of leftover cheesecake from the girls' night out, wrapped in plastic like a secret.

It sat on the shelf like a dare. Like it knew her name.

It glowed like a holy object.

Kayla stood there longer than she meant to, the cold air spilling onto her bare legs. Her stomach wasn't even growling. That was the scary part. She wasn't hungry in her belly.

She was hungry in her spirit.

She swallowed.

"Don't do it," she whispered.

Her voice sounded small in the kitchen, swallowed by the hum of the fridge.

Then she did it anyway.

She pulled the cheesecake out like it was fragile. Like it mattered. She set it on a plate. She didn't cut a "reasonable" slice. She cut a piece that looked like she was feeding grief.

A big one.

She took the first bite and felt it hit her tongue like relief. Sweet.

Dense. Familiar. For two seconds, her shoulders dropped. For two seconds, the world softened.

By the third bite, the relief started to turn on her.

Halfway through eating it, guilt hit her like a brick.

"No, no, no..." she groaned, pushing the plate away so hard the fork clinked against the ceramic and made a sharp, accusing sound.

Her chest tightened.

She hated this part.

The cycle.

The shame that came sprinting behind the craving, like it had been waiting all day for its turn.

She sat down in the kitchen chair, elbows on the table, head in her hands. She didn't text her friends. She didn't cry. She didn't want sympathy or pep talks.

She didn't even want to forgive herself.

She just sat there, hating herself, staring at the abandoned plate like it had betrayed her.

Then her phone buzzed.

She flinched, like it had caught her doing something wrong.

A message from Jakil.

"You ready for tomorrow's session?"

Her stomach twisted in a new way. Not hunger. Not cheesecake. Something sharp and embarrassed.

She stared at the screen, thumb hovering. She could lie. She could pretend it didn't happen. She could show up tomorrow and punish it out of her body like she always did.

But the shame was tired. It didn't want secrets anymore.

She typed.

"I messed up."

She watched the little "delivered" checkmark and felt her heartbeat jump.

Three seconds later.

"What happened?"

She exhaled hard through her nose, almost laughing because the truth sounded stupid.

"Cheesecake happened."

She waited.

Braced herself.

Disappointment.

Judgment.

A lecture.

She could already hear the tone some men used when they wanted to act like your choices offended them personally.

Instead, his reply came and made her blink.

"Okay. How did it make you feel?"

She stared at that sentence like it was written in another language.

He wasn't asking what she ate.

He was asking what it did to her.

She swallowed and typed back the truth.

"Honestly? Like trash."

"Why?"

Kayla's eyes burned, and she hated that. Hated how fast emotion rose when she tried to name it.

"Because I'm trying to do better and I already messed up."

The pause before his next message felt like standing in front of a door, waiting to see if it would slam.

Then it came.

"You didn't mess up. That's normal. You're human."

She stared.

"One slice won't stop your progress."

Her throat tightened.

"But don't hide from me. Come train tomorrow. We'll work through it."

Something loosened inside her chest so suddenly it almost scared her. It wasn't excitement. It was relief. The kind you feel when you realize you're not alone in your mess.

She typed with shaking fingers.

"You sure you're not disappointed?"

His answer arrived instantly, like he'd been waiting for her to ask.

"No. I'd be disappointed if you quit."

A beat.

"But you're still here."

Kayla put the phone down like it was too heavy to hold. She leaned back in the chair and stared at the ceiling, blinking hard. Her eyes filled anyway.

Nobody ever talked to her like that.

Not even her exes.

Not even her friends.

Not even herself.

She wasn't used to someone being firm without being cruel. She wasn't used to accountability that didn't come with humiliation attached.

She wiped her face with the back of her hand and sat there a long time, letting the words settle into her skin.

THE NEXT MORNING, she showed up to the gym wearing an oversized hoodie and a hat pulled low. Not because it was cold, but because she wanted to hide her face. She felt exposed, embarrassed, guilty.

Like a cheesecake sign was written across her forehead.

She stepped inside and the smell hit her first, rubber mats and metal and that sharp clean sanitizer scent that reminded her of effort. Mirrors everywhere. Bodies moving with purpose. People who looked like they'd never eaten cheesecake in their life.

Her chest tightened.

Jakil spotted her immediately.

"Rough night?" he asked gently.

Kayla's eyes flicked away. "Can we not talk about it?"

He didn't push. Didn't tease. Just nodded once, like he understood the kind of shame that didn't want to be held up to the light.

"Okay."

They warmed up in silence, but it wasn't awkward silence.

It was heavy silence.

The kind that has meaning in it.

Still.

Charged.

Halfway through the session, she was doing weighted step-ups, concentrating so hard on her balance that she wasn't paying attention to how tired her legs were. Her foot slipped.

She stumbled—hard.

And before she could catch herself, Jakil grabbed her waist to steady her.

Not her arm.

Not her shoulder.

Her waist.

Kayla froze.

Jakil froze.

Their bodies were close enough for Kayla to feel his breath against her cheek. His hands were warm and strong, fingers spread across her curves like he suddenly realized how soft she really was. Not in a judgmental way.

In a *real* way.

His breath changed. She felt it.

He swallowed.

"You okay?" he asked.

His voice was low, not playful this time.

Not professional.

Something else.

"Yeah," she whispered.

He didn't move his hands immediately.

And when he finally did, he pulled away slowly, like he wasn't sure if he wanted to.

Kayla stepped back too fast, her heart pounding like it was trying to escape her chest.

"Maybe we should take a break," she mumbled, eyes down.

He nodded tightly, rubbing his jaw like he was trying to reset himself.

"Yeah," he said. "Yeah, that's… probably smart."

They both pretended it was nothing.

It wasn't nothing.

The rest of the session, he avoided standing too close. He gave instructions from a half-step farther than before. When he adjusted her form, he used words more than hands. Kayla avoided looking directly at him, afraid she'd see something in his face that neither of them were ready to talk about.

But the air between them had changed.

They weren't trainer and client anymore.

Not fully.

Not after that moment.

Not after that touch.

Not after that heat.

And both of them knew it.

They just didn't say it.

Not yet.

KAYLA DIDN'T NOTICE the change at first.

But other people did.

On Monday morning, she walked into the coffee shop with her usual oversized tote bag, to meet the girls and get her morning Iced coffee. She wasn't thinking about her body or her progress or anything except getting to work on time and to her desk before her boss noticed.

But Jasmine noticed.

She stopped mid-sentence, mouth falling open.

"Kayla… your face."

Kayla blinked, thrown off. "What about it?"

"It's… smaller," Jasmine said, stepping closer, squinting like she was trying to confirm her own eyes. "Girl, you look different."

Kayla frowned, touching her cheeks. "No, I don't."

"Yes, you do," Jasmine insisted. "Your jawline is poking out like it's clocking in for work!"

Sarah overheard and leaned in, eyes sharp and practical. "She's right. Something's shifting."

Michelle popped up from nowhere like she'd teleported, peering at

Kayla like she was an art project. “Let me see.” She squinted dramatically. “Okay, yeah. Yeah! Your face looks snatched.”

Kayla rolled her eyes, but her cheeks warmed. She wanted to dismiss it, but something warm bloomed in her chest anyway.

Maybe she was changing.

Maybe the work was actually doing something.

She still couldn’t see it clearly yet. All she felt was the struggle. The soreness. The treadmill nightmares.

But she carried that warmth with her through the rest of the day.

That afternoon, she walked into the gym with a little more confidence.

Just a little.

Jakil noticed instantly, like he was trained to spot the smallest shift.

“You’re standing taller,” he said.

Kayla scoffed. “No I’m not.”

“Yes, you are,” he said. “I see everything.”

The way he said it made her heart skip, and she hated that it did.

They started the session.

Planks. Rows. Deadlifts.

Her muscles trembled. Sweat slipped down her back. Her breath burned in her throat. The gym noise surrounded them, weights clanking, shoes squeaking, people talking, but Kayla felt like she was in a tunnel, focused on one thing.

Halfway through, she caught her reflection in the mirrored wall.

For the first time in years…

she didn’t look away.

Her face looked different. Slightly slimmer. Smoother. Her posture stronger, like her spine had remembered it deserved space. Her waist —maybe a little more defined. Not perfect. Not finished.

But real.

She stared longer than she meant to.

Jakil stood behind her and spoke softly.

“Do you see it yet?”

“See what?” she whispered, still staring.

"The beginning," he said.

Her throat tightened. "I don't want to get excited too early."

"Kayla," he said, stepping beside her, voice steady, "you're working your ass off. This isn't luck. It's you."

She looked down, overwhelmed, emotional, like she didn't know where to put the feeling.

He placed a hand gently on the small of her back—steady, warm, grounding.

Not too intimate.

Not inappropriate.

Just enough to let her know he was right there.

"You're allowed to be proud," he said.

Kayla exhaled shakily. "It's just… I'm not used to seeing myself change."

"You will be," he said. "And soon everybody else will, too."

She looked up at him then—really looked—and something in his eyes made her breath catch.

Something unspoken.

Something he wasn't supposed to feel.

Something she wasn't ready to understand.

He stepped back, clearing his throat like he was snapping himself out of it.

"Alright," he said, forcing a lighter tone. "Break time's over."

The moment dissolved, but the effect lingered.

Later that night, Kayla stood in front of her mirror at home. She turned sideways. Then the other side. Then straight on.

Her jawline was a little sharper.

Her stomach a little flatter.

Her back a little stronger.

She touched the mirror gently, whispering, "Okay… maybe you can do this."

And for the first time in years…

she believed it.

Not fully.

Not loudly.

But enough.

Enough to keep going.

Enough to hope.

Enough to wonder why her heart fluttered every time Jakil said her name.

She didn't know it yet...but that small spark, was about to grow into something neither of them was ready for.

19

ATTENTION SHE NEVER ASKED FOR

By week three, Kayla had a routine.

Water bottle.

Headphones.

Hoodie.

Deep breath.

Walk into the gym like she belonged there... even if she still didn't fully believe it.

But the gym believed it.

People started noticing her.

Not in the way they noticed the women with perfect abs or designer leggings, but in small, curious glances. Little double-takes. Quiet respect.

She didn't see it.

Jakil did.

He watched from across the room as she warmed up on the treadmill, ponytail bouncing lightly, her face focused, determined, almost fierce.

"She's changing," he murmured to himself.

A trainer passing by said, "New client?"

Jakil nodded. "Yeah."

"She's killing it."

"She is."

He said it with pride he wasn't supposed to feel.

Kayla moved to the stretching area, trying to ignore how sore her body was. As she sat down on the mat, a slim woman wearing bright pink leggings approached Jakil nearby.

"Hey, Jak," the woman purred. "You free later? I need another session."

Kayla didn't mean to listen…

but the woman made it hard to ignore.

Jakil nodded politely. "I'm booked."

She leaned closer. "Maybe after hours?"

He stepped back — just slightly. "I said I'm booked."

Kayla blinked.

Wait.

Was he… uncomfortable?

The woman made a face, rolled her eyes dramatically, and sashayed away with unnecessary hip movement.

Kayla bit her lip, suppressing a smile.

Maybe she wasn't the only one annoyed by gym Barbie dolls.

Jakil walked over.

"You ready?" he asked.

"For what? Watching girls flirt with you?" she teased without thinking.

He smirked. "That doesn't count."

"What doesn't count?"

"That wasn't flirting. That was… pest control."

Kayla laughed — a real, bright one.

For a moment, he looked at her in a way he wasn't supposed to.

Not as a client.

Not as a friend.

Something else.

He snapped out of it quickly.

"Alright," he said. "Let's get to work."

. . .

Today was leg day.

Kayla hated leg day.

By the second set of lunges, her thighs were vibrating like overworked engines. By the third set, she was cursing internally.

"I can't do this," she muttered.

"You're doing it," he said.

"I want to quit."

"Not today."

"I hate you."

He grinned. "You said that last week."

"And I meant it then too."

"Good. Keep going."

She pushed through the burn, face flushed, sweat dripping down her neck. When she finished the last rep, she dropped onto the bench, chest heaving.

Jakil handed her water.

"You killed that," he said.

"No," she panted. "That killed me."

But she smiled.

He loved that smile.

More than he should.

As they moved to the cable machine, another woman walked by — tall, gorgeous, toned, the kind that lived in gyms like she paid rent there.

She glanced at Kayla.

Judged her instantly.

Then smiled sweetly at Jakil.

"Hey, stranger," the woman said, twirling her hair. "You're training her today?"

Jakil nodded. "Yeah."

"Oh," the woman said, looking Kayla up and down… "Cute."

Kayla stiffened.

Jakil's jaw tightened.

He stepped slightly closer to Kayla, his voice calm but edged with something firm.

"She's one of my strongest clients."

The woman's smile faltered. "Oh. Well. Good luck."

Then she walked off, annoyed her charm didn't work.

Kayla stared at him. "You… didn't have to say that."

"Yes," he said quietly. "I did."

At the end of the session, Kayla leaned against the wall, exhausted but glowing in a way she didn't recognize yet.

Jakil handed her a towel and said without thinking:

"You're beautiful when you push yourself."

Her breath stopped.

He froze.

She blinked. "What?"

He cleared his throat, stepping back like he realized he'd stood too close.

"I mean… you're strong. You look strong. That's what I meant."

But that wasn't what he meant.

And she knew it.

Kayla looked at him for a long moment — longer than she normally allowed herself.

Then she whispered, "Thank you."

He nodded, eyes lingering on her a second too long.

It was nothing.

It was everything.

And neither of them were ready to face what was building.

Not yet.

KAYLA DIDN'T EXPECT it to happen so soon.

It was a Thursday morning, two weeks after the last workout that almost broke her, when she stepped into her jeans and paused.

Something felt… loose.

She tugged the waistband.

Tighter last week.

Much tighter the week before.

She blinked hard, pulled the jeans off, and slipped into them again —slower this time, like they were fragile.

They slid up easier.

The button closed without a fight.

Her breath trembled. She didn't smile. Not yet. She didn't trust it.

She grabbed a different pair of jeans. Same thing.

Then another.

And another.

The room grew quiet—so quiet she could hear her own heartbeat.

She stood in front of the mirror, hands gripping the sides of her thighs.

Her stomach wasn't flat.

Her hips were still full.

Her arms still soft.

But something had changed.

Her waist had a curve she hadn't seen in years.

Her cheeks were a little sharper.

Her posture had confidence she didn't realize she'd built.

Her throat tightened.

A small, soft sob slipped out—surprised, grateful, overwhelmed.

She whispered to her reflection, "Oh my God… I'm doing it."

Not for a man.

Not for approval.

Not even for Jakil.

She was doing it because her body finally felt like it was listening to her.

And she hadn't felt listened to in a long, long time.

At the Gym, Jakil noticed the second she walked in.

He tried not to stare.

Failed.

She wasn't wearing anything tight, nothing revealing. Just leggings and an oversized shirt. But the way she carried herself—chin a little higher, steps a little lighter—made him stop mid-conversation with another trainer.

She didn't see it.

He did.

His chest warmed with pride, but also something dangerous, something he'd been trying to hold back:

Desire.

He inhaled slowly, steadying himself.

When she approached, she smiled at him—small but real, the kind of smile that made his pulse trip over itself.

"You ready?" he asked.

"Yeah," she said, trying to sound casual. But her eyes shimmered with something he couldn't quite place.

He glanced at her from head to toe.

Not in a checking-you-out way.

In a *noticing everything* way.

"You look… different," he said.

She swallowed. "Different how?"

He hesitated.

He shouldn't say it.

He knew he shouldn't.

But the truth slid out anyway.

"Stronger. More sure of yourself…"And beautiful."

Kayla's breath caught.

He felt the moment hit her.

Felt it hit him too.

He looked away quickly, pretending he needed to adjust a dumbbell, pretending he hadn't crossed a line.

"Let's warm up," he said gruffly.

Kayla followed him, her hands trembling slightly, her mind spinning.

Beautiful.

Nobody said that to her without a joke attached, or, "you're cute for a big girl."

But he said it.

Soft.

Certain.

Like he meant it.

The warm-up felt easier.

The weights didn't scare her as much.

Her body listened better.

Jakil kept stealing glances he thought she didn't notice.

During squats, her balance was steadier.

During planks, her arms shook less.

During the treadmill cool-down, she smiled without realizing it.

When she finished the last set, sweat dripping, hair messy, cheeks flushed—

Jakil stared at her like she was the most captivating thing in the room.

He didn't say it.

But she felt it.

After the workout, she grabbed her bag to leave, but something stopped her.

She turned to him.

Her voice barely above a whisper.

"Thank you… for not giving up on me."

He blinked.

Hard.

"I never wanted to," he said.

Then, softer: "I don't think I could."

Their eyes held just a little too long.

A world sat between them.

A world neither of them was ready to step into, at least not…

yet.

20

THE NIGHT THEY DON'T PRETEND

After what happen, Kayla workout routines continued. Jakil was playful as usual and caring, as if nothing happened, but Kayla body and emotions told a different narrative. Neither of them talked about it the next day.

Or the day after that.

But it lived between them anyway, in the way Jakil gave her space without pulling away, in the way Kayla felt her body respond before her thoughts could catch up. The gym didn't feel compromised. It felt charged. Like a place that had witnessed something sacred and wasn't about to betray it.

Their sessions continued.

Structured. Focused. Professional on the surface.

But every adjustment carried memory. Every mirror reflected more than form. Kayla moved differently now—not because of what had happened, but because she couldn't unknow herself anymore. And Jakil noticed. Not with hunger. With restraint. With respect sharpened by awareness.

They didn't flirt.

They didn't retreat either.

What had passed between them didn't need explanation yet. It needed time to settle—to reveal whether it was an impulse...

or a direction.

After more workouts, more lingering conversations, more touches that lasted a little longer than they should have—

he asked her out properly.

Not for coffee.

Not to "go over her plan."

Not under the guise of training.

"Let me take you to dinner," he said one afternoon while wiping down equipment.

She blinked. "Like... a date?"

"Like a date."

She should have said no.

She didn't.

Dinner turned into drinks.

Drinks turned into laughter.

Laughter turned into that dangerous closeness where knees touched under the table and eyes kept locking without meaning to.

On the ride back to her place, the car was thick with unspoken things.

"Are you sure?" he asked quietly when they pulled up outside her building.

"No," she replied honestly. "I'm not sure about anything with you."

He let out a broken little laugh. "Me either."

They made their choice anyway.

What happened next belonged to the both of them—messy, tender, intense, confusing. Years of his casual intimacy crashed into her guarded heart, and for once, it didn't feel casual at all.

He hadn't been planning on feeling.

She hadn't been planning on giving that much of herself.

And yet, in the low light of her bedroom, stripped of titles and roles and expectations, they saw each other clearly in a way the world never had.

They moved toward each other without urgency, as if both understood that rushing would break the spell. His hands settled at her waist, thumbs brushing the warm skin there, grounding her. She rested her palms against his chest, feeling the strength beneath—solid, familiar, real. Not a performance. Just him.

When he kissed her, it was slow, exploratory, lips lingering like he was learning her rather than claiming her. She responded by tilting her head, deepening it just enough to let him know she was choosing this. Choosing him. The knowledge softened something in his face.

His mouth traced along her jaw, paused at her ear, his breath warm and unhurried. She shivered—not from anticipation, but from how carefully he paid attention. Every touch felt intentional. Reverent. As if he understood this wasn't just a body in front of him, but a woman standing at the edge of herself.

She guided him toward the bed, fingers threaded with his, and when they lay down, they stayed close—foreheads touching, breaths syncing. His hand skimmed along her back, feeling the curve of her spine, the strength she'd built, the softness she still carried. She pressed closer, fitting into him instinctively, her head settling against the place where his shoulder met his neck.

As time stretched, they explored each other in pieces, hands learning shoulders, mouths lingering at collarbones, fingers tracing familiar paths with new meaning. When he kissed her neck, she closed her eyes, trusting him fully, and when she reached for him, it was with certainty rather than hunger.

The night unfolded in waves—closeness, pause, closeness again—until emotion blurred into sensation and sensation into something deeper. He held her like he was afraid of letting go too soon. She held him like she knew this moment mattered more than whatever came after.

When they finally grew still, she rested against him, her cheek warm on his chest, listening to his heart slow beneath her ear. His arm curved around her waist naturally, protective without being possessive.

For the first time in a long time, he didn't feel restless.

For the first time in a long time, she felt chosen—not for her body, not for her potential, but for exactly who she was in that moment.

And neither of them pretended it was anything less than what it was:

real,

temporary,

and unforgettable.

When it was over, they lay in the quiet, their breathing slowly evening out.

Her head rested on his chest.

His arm draped over her waist.

For a few suspended minutes, it felt like this could be it.

Like this could be the story.

Like he could be the man she ended up with.

He pressed his lips to her forehead.

"Kayla," he whispered.

"Hmm?"

"You're dangerous," he said softly.

"How?"

"Because you make me want to be a man I'm not sure I know how to be."

She didn't respond to that.

Didn't know how.

She just closed her eyes and let herself feel wanted—

not for a night,

but like she'd become part of his world.

Even if some part of her feared,

she would never fully fit into it.

For a while, they existed in their own little bubble.

They didn't call it a relationship.

Didn't define it.

Didn't put labels on it.

But he was the one texting good morning.

She was the one cooking for him after late sessions.

They were the ones stealing kisses between sets and pretending nobody saw.

Her body continued to transform—curves tightening, waist carving, confidence growing.

People stared when they walked into places together.

Some women glared.

Some men took a second look at her, then a third.

Kayla should have felt on top of the world, but underneath her glow, fear lingered.

One night, she rolled over in bed and found him staring at the ceiling.

"What's going on in that head of yours?" she asked lightly.

He hesitated.

"Nothing," he said.

"Liar."

He exhaled slowly. "I'm trying not to mess this up."

Her smile faded.

"How could you mess it up?" she asked quietly.

"By being who I've always been," he said. "By not being enough of what you deserve."

She pushed herself up onto her elbow. "I knew who you were when I started all this, Jakil. I'm not confused."

"Are you sure?" he asked. "Because sometimes I think you see more in me than is really there."

Her chest tightened. "Don't do that."

"Do what?"

"Try to push me away before anything even goes wrong."

He looked at her, eyes heavy with conflict.

"You know I'm not built like a one-woman man," he said. "I'm trying. I really am. But I'm scared that when this... intensity calms down, I'll feel that itch again."

"The itch to what?" she asked, even though she knew.

"To roam."

The word hung in the room like a storm cloud.

She swallowed, heart aching. "Thank you for being honest," she said softly.

"I wish my honesty made me better," he murmured. "Instead of just... clearer."

She lay back down beside him, staring at the ceiling too.

They held hands in the dark, both knowing what neither wanted to say.

Their story had always had an expiration date.

They just didn't know when it would arrive.

IT DIDN'T END with a big fight.

It ended with a quiet conversation

on a Sunday afternoon

at her place.

They had just finished eating.

Kayla sat on the couch, legs tucked under her, wearing one of his t-shirts.

He watched her from the other side of the room, heart heavier than he expected.

"You look different," he said, eyes tracing her new shape.

"I know," she replied. "I feel different."

"You should," he said. "You worked for all of it."

She smiled—but it wasn't carefree. It had weight.

"I know why you're really looking at me like that," she said.

"Why?" he asked.

"Because you know other men are going to start looking at me like that too."

He didn't deny it.

"I'd be lying if I said it doesn't bother me," he admitted.

"But you're not the staying type," she said gently. "And I'm finally becoming the type of woman who deserves someone who stays."

The words were soft, but they cut.

He looked away; jaw tight.

"I don't want to hurt you," he said.

"You haven't," she replied. "Not yet. And I want to keep it that way."

His eyes glossed over. He blinked it away.

"So what are we saying?" he asked roughly.

She took a breath that shook at the end.

"I'm saying I will always be grateful for you," she said. "You helped me see myself. You were the bridge from who I was to who I am now."

"A conduit," he murmured.

She nodded. "A beautiful one. A necessary one. But not the final stop."

He swallowed hard.

"You know," he said, voice low, "I wanted the world to see you the way I saw you long before your body caught up."

"I know," she whispered.

He moved to sit beside her.

"Can I be selfish for one second?" he asked.

"You've earned one," she said.

He cupped her face and kissed her slowly...

Not with the heat that often burned between them,

but with gratitude, regret,

and a strange aching pride.

When they pulled apart, both of them were misty-eyed.

"We'll still be friends," he said, as if promising himself as much as she had promised to remain his.

"We better be," she said, wiping her cheek. "You're not getting rid of me that easily."

They laughed, even as their hearts broke a little.
And just like that, without screaming or slamming doors,
they let each other go.
Not because they stopped caring,
but because they finally cared about themselves, enough
to honor, who they really were.

21

CLOSER THAN EITHER PLANNED

The next few weeks blurred into a rhythm.

Work.

Gym.

Sleep.

Repeat.

Kayla's body kept changing, slowly but undeniably.

Her clothes fit differently.

Her walk shifted.

Her energy felt... lighter.

One afternoon, as she finished a set of cable rows, she caught two guys on the other side of the gym watching her in the mirror.

Not in the mocking way she'd learned to fear.

Curious.

Interested.

One of them said something under his breath and nodded toward her. The other smiled.

Kayla's first instinct was to shrink, to look away, to pretend she hadn't noticed.

But this time, she didn't.

This time, she held the eye contact for half a second before turning back to her movement.

Jakil saw the whole thing.

His jaw clenched.

He didn't say anything, but his next instruction came out sharper than usual.

"Alright," he said. "Let's move to the next one."

"You okay?" she asked.

"I'm good," he replied quickly. "You're doing great. Let's keep going."

They moved through the workout—lunges, presses, curls—but there was an undercurrent to everything now. A charge neither of them mentioned.

During her cool-down, she sat on the edge of a bench, wiping sweat from her forehead.

"Can I ask you something?" she said.

"Ask."

She hesitated. "Why are you doing this? For me, I mean. I get that I'm a client, but… it feels like more than that."

He looked at her for a long moment, like he was weighing how honest he wanted to be.

Then he said, "Because I see where you could be. And I know what it's like to want something more from yourself and not know where to start."

"That's it?" she pressed.

A small, almost sad smile touched his lips.

"And because," he added softly, "I think the world would lose its mind if you ever saw yourself the way I see you."

Her chest tightened.

"You really think I can be… that woman?" she whispered.

"Kayla," he said, voice low, certain. "You already are. We're just taking off the layers that kept you from believing it."

She didn't know what to say to that.

So she just nodded, hoping he couldn't see how deeply those words landed.

They didn't touch.

They didn't flirt.

But something between them stepped one notch closer and neither of them pulled it back.

IT HAPPENED ON A SATURDAY.

Michelle dragged Kayla out to a lounge after weeks of pestering her.

"You've been hiding in that gym, girl," Michelle said. "We're going out. You don't get a vote. Put on something cute."

"Define cute," Kayla muttered.

"Something that shows life is doing what it's supposed to do," Michelle replied. "Don't make me come dress you myself."

Kayla almost canceled.

But when she stood in front of her closet, she saw things differently than she had months ago.

She picked a black fitted dress that had once been too tight, then too uncomfortable, then pushed to the back of the rack.

Tonight, it slid on smoothly.

It hugged her waist.

Framed her hips.

Showed a soft hint of collarbone.

She stared in the mirror, stunned.

She didn't look small.

She didn't look like somebody else.

She looked like herself—
just more defined, more present, more alive.

When she arrived at the lounge, she spotted her friends first. Lisa whistled so loud heads turned.

"Oh. My. God," Lisa said. "Look at you."

Jasmine's jaw dropped. "Okay, waist! I see you!"

Sarah grinned. "Yeah, we're definitely not paying for our own drinks tonight."

Michelle just folded her arms with a smug smile. "Told you. I knew this body was under there. You just needed the right person to pull it out."

At the bar, men noticed.

One guy offered to buy her a drink.

Another struck up a conversation.

A third couldn't stop staring.

This used to be the kind of attention that went straight to her friends.

Tonight, it followed her too.

And though she played it cool, inside, she was shaking.

During the Uber ride home, Kayla stared at herself in the reflection of the window.

She wasn't used to being seen.

Really seen.

It scared her.

It excited her.

It made her think of him.

She pulled out her phone.

Kayla:

I went out with the girls tonight.

jakil:

Yeah? How you feel?

She hesitated, then typed:

Kayla:

Like people are finally seeing me.

There was a longer pause this time.

Then:

jakil:

Good. They should.

Just don't forget who saw you before they did.

Her heart clenched.

She didn't respond.

She didn't have to.

Then came the night that everything tipped. It didn't start out special, just another late session.

The gym was empty, doors locked, lights dimmed, music softer, air cooler. Kayla had stayed late at work and asked if he could push her time back.

"Yeah," he'd said. "I'll wait."

She showed up tired, hair pulled into a messy bun, eyes shadowed with the kind of fatigue that came from working hard on more than just her body.

"You good?" he asked.

"Long day," she said. "But I'm here."

"That's why you're winning."

They did a shorter workout. More stretching. More core. A lighter day.

When they finished, she sank onto the mat, legs extended, leaning back on her hands.

"I can't believe how far I've come," she murmured.

"I can," he said. "I've been watching."

She smiled. "You sound proud."

"I am."

They sat there in silence, the kind that wasn't awkward anymore.

The airflow hummed.

The front desk attendant turned off more lights.

"I'm leaving now Jakil, I'll lock the door behind me."

"Thanks Sharon, have a good evening and be safe."

"I will." Sharon locked the door with that familiar click and rattled the door just to make sure it was locked. Jakil walked to the door to check it, and then waved good bye before rejoining Kayla.

The mirrors that once were filled with images, no longer felt like an audience. The lights were dimmed to a low hum, reflecting the rows of equipment, benches, bars, plates, all stacked with military precision. The air still held warmth, the faint scent of metal, sweat, and clean.

Kayla stood near the mirror, stretching, her reflection unfamiliar even to herself. Shoulders stronger. Waist carved. Thighs firm where softness once lived. She caught him watching—not hungrily, not possessively—but with something like awe.

"You did this," he said quietly.

She smiled. "You helped."

"No," he corrected, stepping closer. "I guided. You chose."

He reached for her then, hands settling at her waist the way they always had—except now his thumbs traced new lines, new strength. She inhaled as if just realizing the body she was standing in. The mirrors caught them from every angle: her posture confident, his frame solid and steady behind her.

THE OUTSIDE SKY had gone completely dark.

"Can I be honest with you?" she asked quietly.

"Always."

"I thought this was going to be about… making men see me," she said. "You know? Like finally being the girl, everybody wants."

"It's not?" he asked.

She shook her head.

"Now it feels more like…" She searched for the words. "Like I'm finally showing up for myself. And that feels better than anybody staring at me."

He watched her, expression soft, eyes dark.

"You have no idea how big that is," he said.

She turned her head and found him already looking at her.

For a moment, everything else disappeared—

the machines, the mirrors, the hum of the building.

It was just him and her.

And the truth between them.

"You know this is dangerous, right?" she whispered.

"What is?" he asked, his voice lower now.

"This," she said. "Us. This connection. You're my trainer. You're… you. And I know your history."

He didn't flinch.

"And you still came to me," he said.

"I did."

He moved a little closer without meaning to.

"And you still trust me with your body," he added.

"With my progress," she corrected. "Let's not get carried away."

He smiled faintly.

"Too late."

Her breath caught.

He reached up and tucked a loose curl behind her ear. His fingers grazed the side of her face, lingering a second too long.

"Kayla," he said softly.

"Yes?"

"You're not just a client to me."

Her heart stopped. Then raced.

"I know," she whispered.

There were a thousand reasons to pull back.

He didn't.

She didn't.

When he kissed her, it wasn't rushed. The kind of kiss that acknowledged space before closing it. Her palms pressed into his chest, feeling muscle shift beneath skin he'd built rep by rep, discipline layered over years. She leaned into him, trusting the hold.

The bench behind them was cool when she sat, his hands still at her sides, grounding her. They moved together with care, like they were aware of where they were—of the mirrors, the equipment, the history soaked into the walls. This place had shaped her body. Now it held this moment too. Jakil kissed her neck slowly, deliberately, lingering at the sensitive hollow beneath her ear. She stopped him.

"Although that feels so good, I need a shower. I'm sweaty, and so are you."

"Then let's take a shower, we have the entire gym to ourselves."

Kayla nodded in agreement without thinking, breath catching—not from heat alone, but from being seen like this. Fully.

In the shadows and the steam from the hot water, Jakil stepped out his clothing completely nude in front of her. Without saying a word, Kayla voice hitched. Her eyes traced every muscle, every refinement and now every inch. He stepped under the water first, not requesting anything of her, while he covered himself with lather from the bar of soap he was using.

Kayla heart was beating so fast she could hardly catch her breath. Slowly she disrobed, as if unveiling a fine piece of art for its very first showing. Jakil eyes framed her, as if they represented a camera lens, taking snap shot after snap shot, trying to find just the right angle to immortalize such a rare object. Then she stepped into the shower behind him, placing her breast against Jakil's back. When he turned toward her

She rested her forehead against his collarbone, water cascading over both of them, and for a moment, the world narrowed to breath and closeness and quiet understanding.

The showers, steam softened everything. Water traced the curves Kayla was still learning to claim. He watched her there, like she was a trophy on display.

When he touched her, hands light, attentive, reverent, it was with appreciation, not urgency—fingers following the lines of her arms, her back, the strength she'd earned.

Soaking wet, Jakil pulled her from the shower into the locker room in front of the full-length mirror where he spread towels onto the floor. Then he positioned Kayla in front of him.

"Look at yourself...your beautiful. This is who I saw the first time I laid eyes on you. Now... you finally get the chance to see, my vision of you."Kayla stares at herself for a long moment without saying anything. Then she begins to speak.

"To be honest Jakil, I never saw me this way. I had settled for someone I didn't really like, someone I really didn't love, isn't that sad?"

"If that were true, I would say yes, but here you are not a figment of your imagination, but a reality. Now just look at yourself, I mean really look. Kayla stared at her complete nude body in the full-length-mirror. Then Jakil begins to kiss her neck. Kayla moans softly. "Don't take your eyes off of yourself. I want you to see you as I do."

Jakil reaches for her breast, holding them both in is strong hands, then kisses them gently one at a time. Kayla closes her eyes.

"Keep your eyes open, I want you to see all the desire I see in you," he demanded. Kayla tries to focus on what the mirror was projecting back at her, but the pleasure in her eyes kept fading to black. The tip of Jakil's tongue roamed ferociously in and out of places with severe hunger, while his fingers played gently in her moist areas.

Kayla could no longer keep her eyes open. Her knees weaken, causing her to sink to the floor.

Jakil continued to feast upon her, licking and sucking without giving her a moment to catch her breath. With complete surrender, she held onto his shoulders, his waist, his face, while he gently guided himself between her thighs, stretching and filling her. With eyes and mouth wide open, she gasps, until his entire length was buried inside. Then he begins to ride her slowly, giving her a moment to exhale, before his movements shifted into a powerful thrust. Kayla looks up in awe of this chiseled statue of a man, that was riding her relentlessly. She watched the lights in the ceiling above him, as his silhouette gyrated from light to darkness.

This is what I wanted; This is what I've been saving myself for. Someone that desires me as much as I desire myself. Give It to me Jakil, give it to me… is something she wanted to scream out at the top of her lungs, but her voice could only whimper with pleasure. Soon something begins to stir inside of her. Something stored miles below the surface. Jakil was positioned on top of her like an oil well rig, digging and digging, now five thousand feet, ten thousand feet, fifteen thousand feet below the surface, until the rig begins to shake. He had finally reached her black gold, and now she was about to explode.

Instantly, Kayla screamed at the top of her voice. Her pleasure echoing off the locker room walls before escaping into the empty gym bouncing off of every mirror, every bench, and every weight until it faded into the silence, but Jakil wasn't finish yet. His prowess not only earned him a reputation of being a great lover, but more than that, he loved the pleasure of pleasing women. Women were emotional, and here in their emotional pocket is where he loved them the most.

Just when Kayla thought she was exhausted and couldn't take anymore, Jakil lifted her off the floor into his arms like she was 20-pound weights. Then he carried her under the steaming shower, where droplets of water soaks her hair. There he put her down standing her up on her wobbly legs before hoisting her up with his forearm into a sitting position against the shower wall, where he dropped her like forty-five pound weights onto his bar-bell again and again until she almost passed out.

FROM THERE HE took her to a bench where he placed towels beneath her. Then he kiss her legs her calf's, and her feet while he continue to fill her with a thirst of pleasure he was trying to quench. In the middle of Jakil making love to Kayla, she whimpers softly, trying to get her words out between his pounding rhythm.

"Why are you loving me like this, she asked?" ...Jakil never stopped his intense motion, instead he raised himself upon the palms of his hand and looks her in the eyes, while burying himself even deeper. Kayla gasp loudly..."Because you deserve to be loved like this Kayla, and if not you, then who?

THE MIRRORS REFLECTED a woman stepping fully into herself, and the man who knew he had been part of her becoming. When they finally broke apart, she was breathing like she'd just finished the fifty yard dash in record time.

In the silence dominated with heavy breathing, they didn't pretend it was simple.

They didn't pretend it would last.

But in that space—built on effort, discipline, and transformation—they allowed themselves to feel exactly what it was, and that was enough.

"WE SHOULDN'T HAVE DONE THAT," she said, voice shaking.

"I know," he replied.

Neither moved.

Neither apologized.

Neither really regretted it.

They just laid there in the silence, knowing there was no going back now.

22

THE WOMAN WHO WALKS IN NOW

Time moved. Not in the dramatic way people like to describe transformation, not with fireworks or sudden awakenings, but quietly, persistently, like the steady ticking of a clock you don't notice until you realize you're late. Days stacked onto days. Weeks folded into months. The kind of time that doesn't announce itself but still leaves fingerprints on everything it touches.

No sweeping eras passed. No before-and-after montage. Just enough time to soften old habits and harden new ones, enough time for resistance to give way to rhythm.

Just enough months for the new version of Kayla to settle fully into herself.

This version didn't arrive all at once. She arrived in fragments. In mornings where Kayla didn't hit snooze. In mirrors she no longer avoided. In the way she no longer apologized for taking up room. This Kayla learned how to sit comfortably inside her own skin, how to recognize herself when she caught her reflection unexpectedly.

She kept training.

The gym became less of a battleground and more of a refuge. The smell of rubber mats and metal, the low hum of machines, the thud of weights hitting the floor, all of it stitched itself into her routine. Training stopped being punishment and started becoming communion.

Sometimes she trained with Jakil.

Those sessions carried their own energy. Comfortable. Familiar. Charged, but controlled. He spotted her without hovering. Corrected without condescension. Watched without staring. There was an unspoken understanding in the way they moved around each other, like two people who knew exactly where the line was and respected it because crossing it would change everything.

THEY JOKED. Small moments. Dry humor. Inside references that belonged only to them. Laughter that cut through tension and reminded her this didn't have to be so serious all the time.

THEY CHECKED IN. Not constantly. Not intrusively. Just enough to let each other know the door was still open.

SOMETIMES SHE WORKED OUT ALONE. And those were the sessions where the real work happened. Headphones in. World muted. Just breath, muscle, sweat, and intention. Alone, she pushed harder. Alone, she learned what she was capable of without an audience.

THEY STAYED in each other's lives—A deliberate choice. One made with awareness instead of impulse, but that boundary held.

Firm. Clear. Protective. It wasn't restraint born of fear. It was discipline born of growth. And Kayla felt stronger for it.

Her body continued to shift.

The changes weren't loud, but they were undeniable. Clothes fit differently. Movements felt smoother. Her body responded instead of resisted.

Her waist cinched.

A subtle curve reintroduced itself, drawing attention without asking for it.

Her arms toned.

Strength visible now, not just felt. Sleeves hugged where they used to hang.

Her face sharpened.

Cheekbones emerged. Eyes brighter. Jaw set with purpose.

But it wasn't just the physical.

That was the surface story. The easy one.

Her walk changed.

No more shrinking. No more tentative steps. She moved like she expected the floor to support her.

Her laugh was louder.

Unfiltered. Unapologetic. The kind of laugh that fills space and doesn't retreat.

Her decisions were bolder.

Less hesitation. Fewer explanations. She chose and stood by it.

One night, the girls went out again.

Not as an escape this time. As a celebration.

Same kind of spot.

Low lights. Plush seating. Bass-heavy music vibrating through the floor.

Same kind of crowd.Familiar faces. Predictable energy. The usual mix of confidence and pretense.

KAYLA FELT it before anyone said it. Like a current humming just beneath the surface.

They walked into the lounge as a unit, but for the first time, eyes didn't just bounce to Lisa or Michelle.

The usual hierarchy faltered. Heads turned twice. Conversations paused mid-sentence.

Eyes landed on Kayla.

Not accidentally. Not briefly.

And stayed there.

Long enough to register. Long enough to linger.

At the bar, a man approached Lisa first out of habit.

It was almost automatic. Muscle memory guided him.

Halfway through his rehearsed line, his gaze slid past her and stopped on Kayla.

Something recalibrated behind his eyes.

"Actually," he said, smile adjusting, "what's your friend's name?"

The pivot was clumsy, but honest.

Kayla's eyes widened.

Surprise flashed before confidence caught up.

Lisa raised an eyebrow, then laughed, genuinely amused. "Her? Oh, that's Kayla. She can speak for herself." She said

sot with jealousy, but with pride.

Kayla recovered, smirking. "I usually do."

The words came easily. Naturally.

He introduced himself. Bought her a drink.

No pressure. No rush.

Stumbled a little over his words when she held eye contact.

That was new. That was power.

It wasn't about him being perfect.

She knew that now.

It was about her finally understanding:

This moment wasn't luck. It was alignment.

She wasn't invisible.

Never had been.

THE REALIZATION LANDED heavy and liberating all at once.

She'd just been dimming her own light to survive.

A survival tactic mistaken for personality.

Now, she let it shine.

Without permission, and without an apology.

Later that night, sitting around their usual booth, her friends couldn't stop staring at her.

Not judgment. Recognition.

"Something is really different," Jasmine said.

Curiosity edged with awe.

"It's not just the body," Sarah added. "It's the way you take up space now."

The words hit deeper than any compliment.

Michelle grinned. "You've always been that girl. The world is just now catching up."Kayla smiled, eyes misting slightly.

Emotion caught her off guard.

"For the first time," she said quietly, "I think I actually believe you."

The confession mattered more than she expected.

They raised their glasses.

A simple ritual. A powerful one.

To friendship.

The constant.

To growth.

The work.

To the woman she became

Not someday. Not eventually.

right in front of them.

Fully present. Fully real.

23

THE MAN SHE WAS REALLY WAITING FOR

It happened on a Tuesday morning.

Nothing special.

No dramatic weather.

No slow-motion scene.

Just a regular day in a life that no longer felt regular.

Kayla rushed out of her building, coffee in hand, bag over her shoulder, phone buzzing with notifications from work. The morning air felt crisp against her skin, the city already awake and impatient. Somewhere nearby, a bus hissed to a stop. Someone laughed too loud. Life moved fast, but she moved with it now.

As she turned the corner toward the train, someone bumped into her hard enough to make her spill a little coffee.

"Oh! I'm so sorry," a deep voice said.

"It's okay," she replied automatically. "I wasn't looking."

She looked up.

He was tall, but not overwhelming.

Warm brown eyes.

Soft beard.

Dress shirt with the sleeves rolled up, messenger bag across his chest.

Not perfect.

Just… real.

For a beat, neither of them moved. Coffee dripped onto the sidewalk between them, steam rising faintly like punctuation.

"You sure?" he asked. "That was my fault. Let me buy you another coffee or something. I owe you at least that."

She started to say no. Habit almost answered for her. Politeness. Speed. Routine.

Then she heard herself say, "Maybe you do."

The words surprised her. They didn't come with nerves. They didn't come with second-guessing. They just… landed.

He smiled—slow, genuine, slightly nervous.

"I'm Devin," he said, sticking out his hand.

"Kayla."

The way he said her name made her smile before she could stop it. Not because of how it sounded, but because of how carefully he said it, like he wanted to get it right.

They walked toward the coffee shop together, conversation stumbling at first, then smoothing out. A missed step here. A laugh there. He didn't rush to impress. Didn't dominate the space. He matched her pace without effort.

He wasn't flashy.

He didn't lead with game.

He asked questions.

Listened to answers.

Laughed at her jokes.

When they reached the counter, he ordered her drink without asking what the cheapest thing was. No hesitation, no side-eye. Just confidence without performance.

"So," he said, holding out her cup. "Can I… maybe take you out sometime? You seem… I don't know. Like you'd make my week better."

She felt a familiar flutter in her chest.

But this one was different.

It wasn't anxiety.

Wasn't fear.

Wasn't desperation.

It was curiosity.

"Maybe you can," she said, taking the cup. "I'll think about it."

"Okay," he said, grinning. "That's not a no. I'll take it."

"Take my number" she said. "We'll see what happens."

Devin fumbles to get his phone.

"Sure, he said"

As she walked away, she felt someone watching her from across the street. Not the kind of stare that made her self-conscious. Something steadier. Familiar.

She glanced up and spotted him—

Jakil, who had left the same coffee shop prior, one he had gotten accustomed to while visiting Kalya. Slung over his shoulder was gym bag.

Their eyes met.

He'd clearly seen everything. The spill. The smile. The exchange. The ease.

Instead of hurt, his face held something else:

Pride.

Relief.

A hint of bittersweet.

He lifted his cup toward her in a small salute.

She lifted hers back.

Across the distance, no words were spoken, but an understanding passed between them.

Thank you.

You're welcome.

We're good.

Then she turned and kept walking.

Not as the girl hoping to be chosen.

Not as the woman defined by who was looking at her.

But as herself—

A woman with a new body, a new life, a new sense of worth…

and a future she finally believed she deserved.

If things worked out with Devin or not, it didn't matter as much as it would have before.

Because no matter who came or went,

she would never again forget the most important truth she'd learned:

She was always enough.

Now the rest of the world just had to catch up.

And somewhere behind her, watching her disappear into the flow of the city,

the man who once thought he was her destination

smiled quietly—

knowing now

he had only ever been the bridge.

HER PHONE BUZZED ONCE MORE as she ascended the steps toward the train's platform.

She paused, sunlight catching the rim of her cup, and glanced down.

A new message.

Devin: "Just making sure that actually happened."

A laugh escaped her before she could stop it.

Kayla: "It did."

A moment passed.

Devin: "Good. Then I'll look forward to whatever happens next."

She didn't answer right away. Not because she didn't want to—but because she didn't feel rushed to define it.

She stepped onto the train as the doors slid closed behind her, the city rolling forward, carrying her with it.

Across the street, Jakil watched the train disappear overhead.

He smiled again.

Not with loss, but with satisfaction.

Because some connections are meant to end exactly where they do, and some beginnings only happen once you're finally ready to meet them.

Kayla stood steady as the train moved, coffee warm in her hand, heart lighter than it had ever been.

A new chapter wasn't waiting somewhere ahead, she was already thriving inside of it.

The End

ABOUT THE AUTHOR

JAY V JONES

A graduate of Columbia College in Chicago, Illinois, Mr. Jones holds a Bachelor of Arts degree in Advertising and Marketing, with minor studies in photography, television production. While at Columbia, he developed a strong foundation in multiple forms of writing, including television, commercial, and screenplay work. His creative skill set spans writing, authorship, video editing, and professional photography.

www.ingramcontent.com/pod-product-compliance
Lightning Source LLC
LaVergne TN
LVHW050649100826
845148LV00011B/2042